The SACRED BAND TRINITY

PART 3 GRAIL

James MacTavish

authorHOUSE®

AuthorHouse™ UK
1663 Liberty Drive
Bloomington, IN 47403 USA
www.authorhouse.co.uk
Phone: UK TFN: 0800 0148641 (Toll Free inside the UK)
UK Local: 02036 956322 (+44 20 3695 6322 from outside the UK)

Published by AuthorHouse 01/30/2021

ISBN: 978-1-6655-8521-7 (sc)
ISBN: 978-1-6655-8522-4 (hc)
ISBN: 978-1-6655-8525-5 (e)

Red Dragon
Sir Galahad
(Richard Allen)
Sir Gawain
(William Wood)
Sir Bors
(Nick Butcher)
Sir Kay
(Karen Milligan)
Sir Gaheris
(Gary Willis)
Sir Bedivere
(Mack Benson)

White Dragon
Sir Lancelot
(Sir Lawrence Worthington)
Sir Tristan
(Tristan Baker)
Sir Geraint
(Geraint South)
Sir Gareth
(Colonel Stephen Thorpe)
Sir Palamedes
(Mohammed Hussin)
Sir Lamorak
(Michael Von Lamorak...dec. WW2)

CHAPTER 1

———❖———

CONTINENTAL EUROPE

8th Century AD

Writings of Sir Galahad – Day 1

W HAT GREATER HONOUR CAN THERE BE THAN TO HAVE YOUR king bestow upon you a task of the gravest importance? I begin these musings from the northern coast of Europe, where I, Sir Percival and Sir Gawain arrived in the middle of the night from the Wessex shores. The seas were mercifully calm, and we arrived without detection, though Gawain noted his concerns about possible Saxon raiders operating nearby. Indeed, we heard coarse shouts in a foreign tongue as we camped by a fallen tree, prompting Percival to extinguish the modest fire he had struck. But the rest of the night passed by uninterrupted.

I've already spent many an hour contemplating the nature of this quest. My king has held his resolve over the years through war, peace or love. It is this very integrity that binds his Knights of the Round Table, the Thirteen, to his service. Knowing not one of us alone could match Arthur's strength has undoubtedly sealed our bond to him and each other. But perhaps also the awareness that should one of us ever dare attempt an act of treason, to truly lead, he would have to be committed to lowering himself to the level of his kin, not soaring above them like an eagle on high. Not one of the Thirteen – even the revered Sir Lancelot – could achieve such a feat. I believe it is this very fact that enables the King of Britons to wield the mighty Excalibur, a weapon so powerful that foes of all creeds cower before it. What would such power be capable of in the wrong hands, I often wonder? Not the sort of thought one cares to dwell upon for too long.

But no one can deny it… our king grows old and is beset with ill health. And increasingly, vivid dreams haunt his beloved Lady Guinevere – dreams of searing pain and anguish, as if Arthur himself had been ripped away from her bosom. We knights know full well our king has called upon the services of the great wizard Merlin for his counsel, the force that forged our trusty blades from the thorns of Avalon, but for reasons unknown, he appears reluctant to interpret the visions our lady has. It is this desperation that has drawn the wizard's young apprentice, she of the wilderness, of deepest green to rival that of the lushest of trees during the height of the sun – Morgan le Fay.

None can question the unequalled talent of this would-be sorceress. Her beguiling charms have certainly turned the heads of many a man, including those in closest company to our king…perhaps even the king himself. For it was she that whispered an interpretation of our lady's dreams into Arthur's ear one night, sharing visions of grandeur and power the likes of which no man has ever witnessed. The ability to not only raze enemies to the ground, but to build upon their bones an empire like no other, one that would never die, surely such a power is irresistible? Such sweet words to an ailing man must have been like nectar to a bee. The very next day, Percival was summoned, and he together with Sir Gawain and I were to travel to the far reaches of the continent in search of the most modest of tokens – a statue. Nothing more.

Writings of Sir Galahad – Day 6

We made good speed across northern Gaul into the heart of the Frankish lands. The king had charged us to stop at Aachen and pay homage to Emperor Charlemagne, a ruler who has been an ally to Britain in the wars against the Saxons. Our host gave us a hearty welcome at court, even preparing a lavish feast in honour of King Arthur and his victories over our common enemy. It came as no surprise, however, to hear the subject of Christianity discussed while seated at the banqueting table, this perhaps being the only stumbling block between our realms. The three of us were warned by Arthur to expect a little politics, being compared to heathens who still worshipped trees and birds over their 'one true god'. Gawain looked distinctly rattled at times, but bit his tongue.

What caught all our attention however was the inquisition regarding our quest itself. It was clear that our host was not wholly ignorant of such mythical wonders, despite his obvious piety. We had sworn an oath to our king not to reveal the true nature of our travels to anyone, but if questioned, to use the cover story of a search for an item of recognisable value to our allies across the continent – the holy cup of life, the 'grail'.

During a moment of more heated debate over the role of religion when ruling, Gawain let slip the name of the sacred statue – known to Morgan le Fay as the 'Palladium' – to a scholar who sat by his side. Both Percival and I heard it. We intervened quickly but feared the damage had been done. Later that evening, as we enjoyed copious wine and mead, the emperor took our ears and shared with us a more intimate perspective. It would appear even Charlemagne's own position on the papacy was not as resolute as one might have imagined, with him too having heard stories of those before him, recounting the rise of the world's greatest empires, including that of Rome itself, and the teat upon which they sucked. He described a maiden, immortalised in stone in Ancient Greece, protected by the Sons of Mars, and long an object of fervent desire by would-be rulers.

The emperor's openness took us all by surprise. It may well have been influenced by the length of the night's festivities, but there was something about an item around the great man's neck that caught my eye. A red jewel, unlike anything I've ever seen, in a sense alive, shimmering brightly with every word spoken by its bearer. Hypnotic.

Writings of Sir Galahad – Day 9

I write now from the borders of Bavaria. A bitter cold atop the teeth of the earth, air fresh but thin. In exchange for stronger steeds, Percival agreed with Charlemagne that we three would divert our route to the Holy Lands and receive a blessing from His Holiness in Rome, Pope Leo III, rumoured back in Britain to be the 'emperor's puppet'. Percival had no intention of losing precious time heading south into Lombardy, instead insisting we move forward across the Kingdom of the Slavs. Gawain had raised yet more concerns about Saxon scouts, as well as the disposition of the Slavs towards strangers… But Percival was certain the emblems of the emperor, granted with honours on our breastplates, would provide a level of protection. After all, the Slavs found themselves squeezed between the swollen empires of both the emperor's Carolingian movement and his rival, the Byzantine. To offend either would surely be a death sentence.

A knight would find it hard not to admire these new gilded breastplates, with intricate blooms wrought in gold against burnished silver, 'stars from the heart' in defiance of any 'Saracen heretic,' the goldsmith called them. My knowledge of the peoples of the East was limited, but enough vitriol was spilt by the goldsmith to suggest it was not just the people of Britain that took issue with the teachings of Rome. Perhaps a greater war was coming, and those of the West considered it wise for all to carefully choose a side now? We therefore rode from Aachen hailed as Paladin Knights, worshippers of the Lord of the Heavens and his one true son, the man they call Christ, to return with the cup that treasured his blood. The title of 'Paladin' perhaps went unnoticed by the court sycophants.

As I write these words, Gawain and Percival are sketching in the gravelly mountain earth potential routes towards the Greek lands. Gawain prefers the more direct route along the Danube, suggesting we would go unnoticed through the valleys and forests. Percival favours the coastal path farthest away from the tribes deep in the continent, a more time-consuming option. A comical argument now breaks out between the two as to what they both have to look forward to upon our return to Britain, Gawain going as far as to mock Percival's abstinence, squared with his own desire to see his adoring maidens once more. Percival mocks Gawain's title 'defender of women', frightened that the knight's bounty will be ransacked in his absence. The two have thankfully now settled their differences. We shall head for the coastal path upon first light.

Writings of Sir Galahad – Day 13

We arrived at the Coast of Dalmatia in the early hours, our progress hindered by uncharacteristically poor weather upon descent from the mountains. After convincing the natives that we were not Slavs or Saracens – our breastplate armour serving us well – an immediate welcome was given to us by the Palace of Diocletian. It is the grandest of courts I have ever cast my eyes upon, pastel orange like the sun itself, and corridors stretching as far as the eye can see. Its name comes from a Roman emperor perhaps more famed for his care of cabbages than his military – in fact, our first meal there consisted mostly of coarse root vegetables and broth, much to Gawain's dissatisfaction!

We had the pleasure of meeting an interesting ship merchant going by the name of Tylos, short in stature, with skin and hair colour far darker than most. He described himself not as Roman or Byzantine, but Phoenician, a people long associated with trade across the Middle Sea. He shared with me his knowledge of the Ancient Greeks and their ways, including tales not dissimilar to those of Charlemagne's court – a Band of warriors fed from the Well of Ares, a citadel known as Cadmea standing proud over the lands of Thebes. I struggle to keep a firm grip on all the names of deities and peoples, especially when these alternate depending on whom you converse with, 'Ares' and 'Mars' for example.

Percival has interjected upon hearing of the Theban culture, clearly having paid more attention to Morgan le Fay's teachings than either myself or Gawain had. He requests more information about this place, and if possible, safe passage across the seas. Tylos agrees in exchange for a suitable remuneration in gold and will take us aboard his vessel in two nights' time. The journey will take near nine days, with stops in several southern ports in places none of us had ever heard of, including Carthage, a ruined city, as well as the northern coasts of the fabled Egyptian tribes. While Percival is insistent that none of us stop or disembark from the vessel at any time, my curiosity is piqued by this great adventure to such lands... and I tell him now, I can make no such promises!

Writings of Sir Galahad – Day 16

The Middle Sea has glistened sapphire blue these past few days, a glorious sight. The weather has been most favourable and Tylos noted he has never seen the waters so calm. He claims the three of us must indeed be 'blessed by the gods' to allow him such a smooth passage. Food has been plentiful, not only with fresh produce collected from Carthage including ripe fruits and meat, but also succulent fish I have now learnt to catch with a line tied to my thorn staff. A morsel of mutton appears to be the most successful bait!

I have found ample time to quiz our seafaring host on his knowledge of the Ancient Greeks and their ways. He tells me of their mighty gods, Zeus, Hera and Hades... but most compelling is Athena, the goddess of wisdom and strength, revered to the point of naming the mightiest city in Greece after her. I whisper a word of the Palladium out of earshot from Percival and Gawain, and Tylos' face freezes like stone. Tales of Cadmus, ruler of Thebes, come to light and the curse of jealousy that was cast upon him by Ares in retribution for the killing of his sacred dragon – an act that would have been seen as noble by us knights. His taking of the fairest maiden Harmonia and the jewel that bears her name were instrumental in Cadmus' downfall. The sacred statue of Athena was taken by others eager for empires of their own, from Alexander the Great to Julius Caesar himself – legends that had made their way into historical texts as far away as Britain, and were immortalised in many a mosaic. I wonder whether Morgan le Fay knew of these deeds as she urged our own king to pursue this quest, and whether she brought its consequences to his attention. It would appear that both this statue and this Necklace are fatefully entwined: to possess one is to possess the other, to rise only to fall. A cycle witnessed by the likes of Tylos and his Phoenician kin, but not yet learnt by so many others. In a few days, we three will perhaps witness and take part in a similar fate.

Writings of Sir Galahad – Day 21

The soft white sands of eastern Greece greet our sea-weary legs as Tylos bids us farewell after seven nights. His skilful piloting between many islands landed his ship at Sounion, just southeast of Athens. At the temple Tylos offered a libation to the God of the Oceans, Poseidon, for our safe passage and urged us to travel north for approximately two nights to reach the Theban lands and the Citadel of Cadmea. I asked how we would know when we've reached these lands, to which he simply replied, 'How all great men have known.' I could not decipher whether this was praise or warning.

During our final night together, Percival was more engaged in Tylos's tales and asked more about these Warriors of Ares, and whether they would pose a threat. Tylos went on to explain that these soldiers were actually born out of love, not war, but how such connections to one another could bring about the fiercest of human impulses. He gave the example of Gawain and his love of women, and what our own king would be prepared to do protect our Lady Guinevere. Such visceral impulses even the sterile Percival could comprehend. That said, Tylos proceeded to relate that no such warrior had been written of since the times of Philip II of Macedon, father to Alexander the Great, who seemingly wiped them out after a battle referenced as Chaeronea. Percival took some comfort in this, but remained resolute and begged me and Gawain to take nothing for granted.

As a parting gift, Tylos presented us with three steeds. We ride to Cadmea upon first light.

Writings of Sir Galahad – Day 23

Navigation of the Greek lands proved trickier than we first thought, made all the worse for blazing heat beating down upon our armour like a mace. We rationed our water stores, and a few rivers along our route offered welcome refreshment, but our usual stoicism had been sapped from us like blood from a smitten boar. It was at dusk when a weary Percival pointed to the ominous shadow of a mound belching up through a layered sky. Sitting proudly atop it were the remnants of what appeared to be a place of worship. The land was not however completely abandoned, with the flickering of lights pooled in the distance suggesting this was still an inhabited region of Greece. Gawain insisted we first search for water and shelter from any locals before attempting to enter the ruins, but Percival overruled him on the grounds that anything either precious or sacred held within these crumbling walls would likely be protected, and the element of surprise was on our side.

The citadel itself bore the wounds of war. Carvings in many languages punctuated each rock and wall. None were clear, but the freshest appeared to be that of a Romulus Augustulus, known in Britain as the Last Emperor of Rome. His torn banner hung over an entrance, all that remained visible that we could translate with our modest Latin being *'circulus finis'* – the circle ends.

Perhaps it was just me, but the concept of an endless cycle of empires and their demise struck me as a threat more than ever before upon reading this. Why would a great emperor choose to relinquish such a power? Had he had his fill of cautionary tales that perhaps had since manifested as pure fiction, only to become reality, so that the thought of being just another power-hungry ruler was enough to wrench himself away from any such temptation? Was it true also, that such contemporaries as Charlemagne had yet to heed this valuable lesson? Could the same be said of our own King Arthur and Morgan le Fay?

Still. I couldn't stop Percival and Gawain from prising open the sealed entrance, pushing hard and lifting the fallen boulders with a grimace to reveal a small passageway. As night settled in, we trod carefully down a stone path to an opening which revealed a small pool of water, milky grey, with only the slightest trickle of feed from the soils above. All three of us were parched, and Gawain was the first to dip his hand into the pool, scoop up a palm-full of water and down it in greedy gulps. At first he appeared fine, and beckoned both Percival and me over to quench our thirst. I took a few cautious sips, only to feel a burning sensation like no other, which disappeared as quickly as it came. Gawain suffered the same reaction, which he described as a vision of brightest blue flame searing from behind his eyes, and what sounded like men's cries from all around the chamber. I too heard these cries, but could not connect them to any particular loved one or close companion. The pain, however, was as if all I ever dared care for was ripped from me in an instant. Upon seeing this most frightening reaction in us, Percival declined the waters.

It was, however, Percival who spotted high up upon a ledge the slender statue of a female, small but detailed. Bathed in the pale light filtering down from above ground – the Palladium. It was he that reached for it and grasped it firmly before raising it high above his head proclaiming, 'My fellow knights, I give you, for King Arthur and Britain, the Grail!'

I write this entry in the comfort of the home owned by a welcoming local in Thebes, warmed by a roaring hearth and red wine. The local knows not of our doings here, only that we are travellers from the West and on pilgrimage to the Holy Lands, her reverence for another goddess named Hestia compelling her to give us shelter for the evening. I watch my fellow Knight Percival, clutching his satchel tightly with the treasure within, wondering what it is we have done.

CHAPTER 2

—————◇◆◇—————

CARDIFF, WALES

29th February 2012 AD

T HE MORNING WAS FILLED WITH COPIOUS AMOUNTS OF CAFFEINE for Luke, now on his fourth cup of coffee, pressing every last drop out of the granules in the cafetière. He'd spent the last few hours staring intensely at the short wooden staff now in his possession. The mighty Excalibur, the sword of legends and fairy tales, only a few hands worthy to touch it, arguably answering to no one. Yet here he was, a man of twenty-six, until the previous summer happily settled in Boston with a doting mother and close friends, now seated at a rickety breakfast table with a cheap gingham cloth, holding a weapon of unrivalled power. Given to him by his not-so-dead girlfriend, who was now some sort of elemental spirit living in the Forth River! He pressed his palms deep into his eye sockets – no wonder his head hurt so much!

'I don't think staring at it will make it reappear as a blade.' Violet said, coughing slightly as she battled the splattering frying pan, attempting to cook eggs.

'No kidding!' Luke replied through a yawn.

Her father had immediately contacted a fellow pub owner following the events at Edinburgh and Arthur's Seat, knowing that a return to The Bear in Bath would be too risky. In the months after the passing of Violet's mother, Nick Butcher had become close with another cancer widow, a lady by the name of Beth. During the treatment of their spouses at Cardiff Hospital they'd spent many an hour in support groups for families impacted by the awful disease, eventually deciding that more value could be found in working as a pair when it came to emotional support. Beth lost her husband three months before Nick lost his wife. Both being pub landlords, they shared advice on running such a business single-handedly. Their mutual co-operation had allowed both establishments to continue trading, flourishing even.

Beth had welcomed the Butchers to The Blue Hare pub on the outskirts of the City. Nick quickly put himself to good use pulling pints while Violet turned to cooking, not her forte, but she'd always been a fast learner. She prided herself on making a mean bacon, lettuce and tomato sandwich and was pleased to report that no customer had contracted food poisoning yet. Both Adam and Luke had joined them under the instructions of Gary, who had wisely decided that it was better for the Red Dragon contingent to split up, to avoid detection by Sir Lawrence and Lady Morgan. Gary had a small house near Newport overlooking the Severn Estuary, and was providing shelter for Graham McCready and his protégé Fernando. Tearing Graham away from his beloved Scottie's bar was hard, but the circumstances were that extreme, and his broader connections within the Sacred Band were needed now more than ever. Such an asset Gary and Nick could not afford to lose to the White Dragon.

'Have you tried to wield it at all?' Violet continued. Luke just shook his head. 'Why not?' she pressed.

Truth was, Luke was too frightened. Just gazing upon the smooth grain of the staff sent an uncomfortable shiver down his spine. He thought of Mary, possibly trapped forever in a state of purgatory, not knowing if she was in pain or still wrestling with any sense of anger or guilt. This, combined with the sword's destructive effects on a sorceress as powerful as Lady Morgan, was enough for him to consider throwing the damned object back in the river and be done with all this nonsense once and for all.

It was only Mary's words that were stopping him. Why was he worthy? Why not his brother Adam? Surely a more suitable candidate and with the same bloodline, from the most noble Sir Galahad? The word 'sacrifice'. Surely, he was not the only one with experience in that department, everyone had lost or given up something. Nothing was adding up.

Violet shoved a plate of toast and her best effort at fried eggs in his direction. 'Eat something!' she instructed. Luke tested her concoction with his fork before taking a bite. 'I suppose it's quite fitting that you now have a sword… given Richard lost his. My dad often said a Knight of the Round Table would sooner part with his life than his sword!' she smiled.

Luke chewed on a tough piece of toast. 'You must have had some weird bedtime stories when you were growing up,' he said flippantly.

'Actually, they were great.' Violet recalled. 'Both Mum and Dad did away with all that prissy princess-in-a-tower rubbish, waiting to be saved by a handsome prince on a white horse, slaying a troll and so on. They got right to the point. Knights were about honour, loyalty and of course – adventure!' she beamed.

'Well… they've not let you down there,' Luke replied. Violet gave a mild chuckle.

'How's Adam?' she enquired.

'You're asking me?' Luke rolled his upper lip. 'Tried to talk to him, but he's not having it right now.'

'You've both lost someone close. Surely he gets that?' Violet proposed.

'I don't think losing Iain was the same as me and Mary,' Luke said. He cleared his plate and dumped the dishes in the sink. 'Mary and I often fought, but never to the death!'

Violet nodded in appreciation, then heard what sounded like the back door click open, only to be slammed shut in a tantrum. Adam's heavy footsteps echoed up the stairwell, he breezed past the kitchen and headed straight for his room. Violet and Luke turned to one another and shrugged.

'You should really try, Luke.' Violet said with concern. Luke stared at the floor, trying not to engage, but gave in to her. With a huff he followed his brother.

∽◎∾

Luke knocked on the bedroom door, trying to be heard over the blaring sound of New Order from within. He shouted Adam's name twice, no reply. Eventually, he just entered uninvited. Adam was sweaty from his morning run, headphones in despite ambient music playing, grinding out press-ups robotically.

'Adam – you want breakfast?' Luke said lightly. Adam gave his brother the courtesy of a pause in his routine to reply with a sharp 'No' before continuing. Luke scratched his head, looking for a reason to remain in the room. 'Do you… do you want me to spot you or anything?' he tried again. Adam deflected laconically once more. Luke knew he had only one option, and that was to throw himself in at the deep end here.

'Look bro… you've barely spoken a word since Edinburgh. Not to me, or Violet. Not even Gary and Nick.' Luke crouched by his side.

'I spoke to Gary yesterday,' Adam retorted, reaching for a towel to wipe the beads of sweat from his forehead.

'And?'

'And… what? He's working with that Carl Bishop friend of his from the York Post and trying through his journalist contacts to follow up on leads for the White Dragon and any related activity. Graham is busy extending his network of Sacred Band members. He said he'll keep in touch with any further developments but until such time, we should keep our heads low. What more do you and Violet want?' Adam snapped.

Luke recoiled. 'Ok, sounds good. All good.'

'We done?'

'No. Not really.'

'Well... I am.' Adam resumed a press-up stance just as Luke put his hand on his shoulder.

'Adam, look. Will you at least talk to me? I know it must have been tough having to do what you did, with Iain and all...'

Adam bolted upright, his face grew cold. 'You're telling me you know how it was? How I felt? Is that it?' he bristled. 'You don't, Luke, you haven't the slightest idea. So don't try and counsel me now that our father's gone, OK?'

Luke's short temper was now starting to fray. 'So, that's it, is it? Now that Dad's gone it's just you and the Red Dragon against the world? Sure, that's exactly what he would have wanted,' he shot back.

'Hey, you're the one with Excalibur! Why aren't you out there defending us all?' Adam fired back.

'Oh, so you're jealous? Jealous that I got the sword and you didn't? Well, I'm sorry! Sorry that it's such a burden on you and what you think is your destiny – to avenge our dad and defeat all your enemies. Ever thought that attitude is the reason why Mary didn't give you Excalibur? Because you just can't be trusted right now?' came Luke's bitter response.

'That and the fact I wasn't both sleeping with her and cheating on her at the same time perhaps? Her way of getting her own back I suppose!' came the lowered tone of Adam. Such a remark was enough to have his elder brother wrench him to his feet by the scruff of his T-shirt and slam him into the far wall, his strength catching Adam by surprise.

'Don't you *ever* talk about Mary that way. You hear me!' the exchange was interrupted by Violet poking her head around the doorframe.

'Sorry to intrude boys... I could hear this was all going so well. Luke, my dad wants to know if you're ready for some more training? You know how persistent he is,' she chirped with her unique blend of sincerity and sarcasm. Luke relaxed his grip and patted Adam's arms apologetically. A crestfallen look from his brother acknowledged his own ill-advised behaviour.

'Thank you, Violet. I'll be right down.'

CHAPTER 3

———◇◦◇◦◇———

LONDON, ENGLAND

29ᵗʰ February 2012 AD

'I'M SORRY GERAINT... WHAT EXACTLY DO YOU MEAN BY ALL OF this?' Sir Lawrence rubbed both his temples in an attempt to control his irascible outburst. 'You're saying we now need to wait until June before we complete our mission? June?' he shrieked.

Geraint South tipped his head down and switched the projector screen off before taking a seat next to Lady Morgan. 'I appreciate it appears frustrating, Sir Lawrence, I do. All my research, however, does indicate that for our lady to truly access the full power of the Grail, it must be on the night of the Venus transit – this year, that means the fourth of June.' He scurried through some scattered papers across the polished wooden desk, seizing parchments at random and waving them under Sir Lawrence's chin.

'You see here, an account as far back as Pythagoras, the recognition of Venus as being both the Morning and Evening Star – the beginning and the end. Then here, more recently in 1763, King George III requested the completion of the King's Observatory here in London in order to witness the event... some scholars suggesting that the event held sway over the expansion of a great empire, or as they would put it, the creation of a new world.'

Sir Lawrence continued to look unimpressed, turning to Lady Morgan for advice and support. Quietly she took one of Geraint's papers and studied it, then turned the corner of her mouth up with a chuckle.

'The number of missed opportunities. Never quite having the right pieces, in the right place, at the right time. We cannot afford to be so reckless once again.' She gently placed the paper back in front of Geraint. 'Somewhat poetic that the strongest of the deities should recognise the power of the female over the birth of new worlds – Athena, then Aphrodite, or Venus as she was known in Latin, and of course, my own sister.' She smiled in thought. 'And should we indeed wait... wait until this opportune time, Sir Geraint, where exactly should we be?'

Clearing his throat, Geraint pulled out a current world map and unrolled it. He crudely drew two thick black lines with a board pen, partitioning large swathes of North Africa, the Middle East and Asia. 'The transit should be visible from anywhere within this stretch of the earth. So, in theory, you could attempt to perform the ritual from any point of your lady's choosing,' he replied.

Lady Morgan leaned over the map and ran her finger back and forth before firmly landing it on a particular spot. 'Here, I think,' she suggested. Sir Lawrence politely pushed her hand aside to study the site.

'Is that... Egypt?' he questioned.

'Indeed it is, my love. The Sinai Peninsula to be precise, I believe?' She turned for confirmation to Geraint, who nodded.

Sir Lawrence was familiar with the area only from the Bible – home of Mount Sinai, upon the summit of which Moses received the famous Ten Commandments, and recognised by several faiths including Judaism, Christianity and Islam. Certainly a location of significance, but uncomfortably exposed.

'Are you sure? Morgan, I understand the importance of this event you, to all of us... but perhaps somewhere more discrete would be sensible...' Sir Lawrence attempted to sway her. Lady Morgan, however, displayed little more than a flicker of emotion and simply picked up the remote for the television intercom. She pressed the power button hard to reveal the stern face of Mohammed Hussin, bristling black beard overgrown, hair unkempt.

'Sir Hussin, thank you for joining us at such short notice once more. How are things in Jordan?' Lady Morgan asked.

'Far less interesting than activities in Britain of late, I hear,' Hussin replied with a raised eyebrow, clearly up to speed with the White Dragon's recent exploits in Edinburgh.

'Ah yes, very true I'm sure. And our treasure, Sir Hussin?' Lady Morgan continued.

'The Palladium is safe and well, Lady Morgan,' Hussin replied. 'I, of course, await your instructions as agreed.'

There was a sharp intake of breath from Sir Lawrence, along with a flashing look of disdain towards his wife. At what stage of the proceedings had she assumed complete command of this engagement? Firstly, handing the prized Palladium over to Mr Hussin without consulting him, now making arrangements behind his back? He grumbled under his breath as he slowly resumed his seat.

'That's wonderful news, Mohammed. You've done the great Knights of Palamedes proud. Sir Geraint South was just briefing my husband and me on the significance of the transit of Venus, which approaches on the fourth of June. I would very much like to clear a path to a specific site just south of your current location. Can you and your men ensure such a welcome for us when the time comes?' Lady Morgan purred.

With a protruding of his jaw and a furrowed brow, Hussin agreed to the request. The timing was generous at eight weeks, with little else expected of him other than to simply prepare for their arrival. That being said, with the scars of previous encounters with the Red Dragon still fresh, Hussin wanted reassurances. 'Are we expecting any additional company, M'lady?' he asked heavily.

'Almost certainly,' came Lady Morgan's frank response.

'And might I ask how the search for Excalibur is going?' Hussin questioned further. Sir Lawrence gave an incredulous glance in Geraint's direction.

'The Trinity will be complete. Trust me,' Lady Morgan reassured, never breaking eye contact with Hussin, aside from a quick glance to the corner of the screen where she detected a sudden movement. 'Why, Sir Hussin, are you not alone in these discussions?' she queried. Hussin turned to look over his shoulder, then muttered something swiftly in Arabic and gestured to the second individual to leave. A young woman, no older than in her mid-teens, Lady Morgan guessed, appeared sheepishly in the background – hazel eyes, warm face, hint of black hair, as dark as Hussin's, slightly braided with beads. A small gold trinket sparkled from her neck – a hand of Fatima symbol. She caught the eye of Sir Lawrence before she left.

'Who was that?' Sir Lawrence asked anxiously.

'My daughter, Aisha. My apologies... She knows she's not meant to be in here when I'm working.' Hussin bowed. Sir Lawrence relaxed a little, although still noticeably vexed by the apparent lack of conscience from his fellow Knight.

'Not to worry, Sir Hussin – always a pleasure to meet the future generation of Palamedes. My, hasn't she grown!' Lady Morgan lightened the tension.

'Both in years and in wisdom, M'lady.' Hussin smiled.

'Well, do be sure to let her know her of father's prestigious place in our ventures... for it will be she that will inherit. Albus Draco.'

'Albus Draco.' Hussin acknowledged.

Lady Morgan closed with a smile of her own. She handed the debate over to Geraint and ushered Sir Lawrence out of the room.

'A little concerning, don't you think?' Sir Lawrence snapped as he closed the meeting room door behind Lady Morgan. The recent family lineage of Hussin had been notoriously fickle, on occasion reneging on allegiance to the White Dragon in favour of their own agenda for power in the Middle East. Now was certainly not the time to be introducing a new generation... especially a young lady who, if anywhere near as headstrong as her father, might just disrupt things at the most inconvenient of times. 'I wasn't even aware he had a child?'

'You need to keep a closer eye on your brethren, my love,' Lady

Morgan soothed with her hand placed across Sir Lawrence's cheek. 'Mohammed introduced Aisha to us on her first birthday if you recall. You were no doubt too busy with work to notice. Always been your weakness, never being present,' she mocked calmly.

'You didn't say anything about Excalibur, Morgan. Why not? You know we don't have it,' Sir Lawrence expressed with concern. 'The Trinity is not complete without it... you know that.'

Lady Morgan smoothed out the creases in Sir Lawrence's collar. 'I believe Excalibur may well come to us, my love. No immediate need to chase the Red Dragon just yet,' she noted.

'Morgan. This is not like the Palladium, where the Necklace of Harmonia can act as your guide or magnet. This is Excalibur. Such rules of attraction do not apply,' Sir Lawrence reminded.

'I am aware of that, Larry.'

'Then what makes you believe the Red Dragon will bring the sword to us... exactly when we need it?'

Lady Morgan clasped Sir Lawrence's hand and inspected the silver ring with the White Dragon inscription upon it. 'Let's just call it faith, shall we. That, and the naivety of youth.'

CHAPTER 4

—❖—

CARDIFF, WALES

29ᵗʰ February 2012 AD

Notes from Carl Bishop – 29ᵗʰ February 2012

WHICH ARE REALLY THE GREATEST EMPIRES? THOSE WHICH cast the largest influence? Was it the British? The French? The Romans or Greeks? All global powers yes, some with a reach from the rising to the setting of the sun... but in most cases, unable to grasp what had truly fuelled them in the first place. Faith.

Since the earliest civilisations, there was always a belief in gods and goddesses. People have been prepared to live and die for them, fight and bleed in their name. It is perhaps this very passion from mankind that keeps such deities alive, their need to be adored above all else. When such passion wanes, the purpose of the deity becomes history, obsolete. It strikes me as most strange to even contemplate such a notion, as a boy growing up in the household of a vicar, attending church as a family every Sunday and being constantly reminded of the presence of the Christian God and his Son being the cornerstone of my existence. My parents weren't to know I would eventually become a journalist, whose very role is to question that which should not be, to challenge and investigate, not just accept events as mere fate or faith.

With my newfound friends here in Cardiff, I have begun to contemplate the concept of a trinity. A rule-of-three does appear to exist in so many of the world's faiths. From Christianity to Judaism, Buddhism and Paganism, the idea of a cycle – birth, life, death – has somehow woven itself into all. Of course, this would make sense from the perspective of us mere mortals. We are born, we live, we die. What else is there to life? Perhaps not a path well understood by our immortal counterparts. To have blood in your veins is a precious thing, knowing that from the moment it flows, time is short.

Christians have recognised the Holy Trinity. You see it also in the Hindu Trimurti – creation, maintenance and destruction. The three jewels of Buddhism, rooted in construction, activity and grace. Freemasons have the three pillars of wisdom, strength and beauty, as well as the symbol of the pyramid. Taoism has its three pure ones. There's even a hint of a triune representation in the Quran, although that's still the subject of debate, I hear from friends.

While many interpretations exist, my passion for mediaeval French literature and Le Morte d'Arthur of Thomas Mallory cannot leave my mind. Most scholars state that the myths surrounding King Arthur and his fabled knights focus on the search for the Holy Grail, or Sangreal as some writers call it. While heavily romanticised and almost certainly embellished over the centuries, Arthurian legend suggests that the King of the Britons himself, as a possible mortal facing inconceivable odds from invading foes, might have had a leap of faith of his own. With the spread of Christianity across Europe at the time, the idea of an object that was used both to drink wine from at Christ's last supper with his disciples and to collect the blood of Christ himself, that could transform the course of a war if taken away from your enemies, could have sounded tempting. Here was a faith undoubtedly seen as an enemy of the indigenous folk of Britain, why wouldn't you challenge it? Find its beating heart and rip it from its bosom?

Now I go further. Imagine you are the King of the Britons, and you come to hear of a sacred object that could secure your kingdom and its future – even expand it to the farthest corners of the known world. A tempting venture, I'm sure one would concur. The Palladium of Ancient Greece, sacred to Athena the Goddess of Wisdom. Capable of granting its bearer an empire, and you alone to wield the mighty Excalibur to defend what you have earned for an eternity.

But there's a problem. The Palladium might give birth to your empire, and Excalibur be there to defend it, but King Arthur was still a man, a mortal. What if he could live forever? Not just be confined to parchments of history and legend? A true, living god. Whispers of a third item may have reached him, perhaps from poisonous advisers like the witch Morgan le Fay, with insatiable ambitions of their own. As with Harmonia herself, wife of Cadmus in ancient Thebes and daughter of Ares, God of War, the Necklace would have granted its wearer ageless beauty and cunning. In the hands of a powerful sorceress and with the teachings of the great Merlin... truly a nigh-unstoppable foe.

I've learnt from my studies of the Round Table and its knights that some of its founders might well have travelled to continental Europe during the eighth century. Again, if Mallory is to be trusted, it was understood that three of the knights who had vowed allegiance to King Arthur were sent on a quest for what we now call the Holy Grail. What if this was the Palladium, which had last been seen in Ancient Greece when the fall of the Roman Empire was imminent? Sir Percival the Virgin, Sir Gawain, nephew to the king, and of course, Sir Galahad, son of Sir Lancelot. These names I believe live on today in my newly found friends, quite possibly descendants from other dutiful Knights of the Round Table. Just like their ancestors, they are at war for what they consider best for their people. I grapple with the idea that over the years mankind has still not let go of its thirst for conflict, always baring its teeth at the sight of a difference in opinion or belief. It is potentially reassuring to know that some aspects of life always remain constant.

The great Sir Percival dies a virgin and has no heirs. I am left wondering what led him to such a path of isolation and loneliness.

Was it a duty to King Arthur? Perhaps guilt that as leader of such a quest he had precipitated the downfall of the kingdom? Did Morgan le Fay corrupt his mind along with that of at least half of the Round Table knights? A martyr perhaps, never wishing to take either side, and prepared to sacrifice for both what I've come to know as the Red and White Dragon factions. A lesson learnt from his travels to Europe and a new form of faith. Unsure. Not much is known other than poetic prose here of course, but it wouldn't be too much of a stretch for an inspired journalist, let alone centuries of inflated folklore.

Enter Sir Galahad and Sir Gawain, the two remaining knights from the quest. Two pillars of unshakeable loyalty to King Arthur and his wife Guinevere, despite the foretold affair between her and fellow knight Lancelot. A doomed affair that both Galahad and Gawain must have known would have torn their kingdom apart, even without the use of magical necklaces that fuel lust and greed. I see many of these loyal qualities in the company in which I have now found myself, and the details shared by Richard Allen and William Wood. I can draw my own conclusions here. For the Allen family, the father's fight has been taken up by his sons, the line of Sir Galahad continues in its indefatigable devotion even now, long after the blood spilt during the battle of Camlann – if indeed this is the source of the legend.

Adam Allen, however, interests me the most. He speaks of another power, older than Arthur's, and connected to warriors before the establishment of Britain. The Kingdom of Thebes and its founder Cadmus. A Band three hundred strong, all in partnership, all male. Sworn by oath to protect Cadmus and his wife Harmonia, but more so their true lady, Athena Pallas. The Palladium is their burden. Sons of Ares, God of War, formidable alone but near unstoppable when paired – such is love. Last heard of at the mercy of King Philip II at the Battle of Chaeronea, Philip's son Alexander dealing the final blow, wiping out all three hundred, as they would have wished. Eventually, Alexander would conquer the known world and found one of the earliest empires the world has ever known. The Palladium's power on full display for all that followed. Its counterpart, the Necklace of Harmonia, once again playing its sister role in their downfall.

While Adam is mindful of his words around company, his elder brother Luke speaks frequently for him. He speaks of his pain at losing his partner, an Iain Donnelly, last year during their encounter at Arthur's Seat in Edinburgh. A pain too complex to understand, that much is certain. Two warriors destined to fight and die beside one another, only to find their objectives opposed. A cruel twist in what it is to be a part of the Sacred Band of Thebes.

I confess to thinking too much now. My study of Mr Mack Benson in York and my close connection to Mr Gary Willis of the Bath Chronicle should be my focus. Whatever this story unfolds, it is clear to me that my own obsessions have for once yielded positive results. I say positive, but the more I uncover from this world of knights, magicians, sacred relics and trinities the more uncertain I become of humanity and its fate.

CHAPTER 5

CONTINENTAL EUROPE

8th Century AD

Writings of Sir Galahad – Day 36

THE LANDS OF BAVARIA HAD PROVEN FAR MORE CHALLENGING ON our return journey. Blasts of frozen air harnessing the strength of a dozen oxen hampered our path back down the rocky summits into the Frankish lands once more. Gawain had been complaining of a sore that had spread from his ankle up to his knee, possibly frostbite. This prompted a return to the court of Charlemagne for immediate treatment.

Percival himself was keen to return to our generous hosts – whether this was for Gawain's benefit or simply to gloat about our success in the eastern provinces and to share a glimpse of the treasured Palladium I wasn't sure. Still, we as Paladin Knights were welcomed again by Emperor Charlemagne and invited to stay the night. The evening's festivities of gluttony and dance took an unexpected turn when our host's eyes glimpsed the tip of the statue protruding from Percival's satchel. It was as if Charlemagne's fingers were possessed as they inched further towards the Palladium, only to be swiped away by Percival. I held my breath as the two rose to their feet, fearing a confrontation that surely would have ended in all three of us being sentenced to death. This mercifully never came to pass – not quite anyway.

An accord was agreed between the emperor and Percival – a duel between his blade and that of the emperor's finest knight. The victor would get to keep the Palladium. Much to my and Gawain's astonishment, Percival raised the stakes further, stating that should he win, he should be awarded not just the Palladium, but the ruby-red jewel around our host's neck. Whatever power this jewel had, it had clearly caught the interest of Percival, who had been acting out of character ever since our success in obtaining the sacred statue in Greece. He would barely eat, barely sleep, clutching the token each night, as if to lose it would break his soul beyond repair. Strange to think he would wager this treasure for the sake of obtaining another, but he was adamant.

Charlemagne's champion knight was summoned. A fair-haired boy, I guessed no more than a score of years old, who had been sitting attentively by the emperor's side for much of our meal. Slim in build but light of foot, armour dazzling without so much as a scratch. His movement to the centre of the banqueting hall silenced all around, aside from a sharp intake of breath from a young man of similar age who had been sitting to his left for the entire evening, never letting go of his hand. Percival did not use his own sword, nobly aware that its magic would likely tip the scales in his favour. He chose a regular broadsword from the armoury. Both knights were without their helmets and equally exposed.

As the bout began, it became clear Percival had underestimated his opponent. Despite Percival having the upper hand in experience, the young knight fluidly danced around our leader for much of the engagement. His sword came dangerously close to dealing a fatal blow across the throat of Percival. For every hard and heavy swing Percival threw, the court champion countered with three or four smaller but better-timed blows, one splitting the pauldron and forcing Percival to bend a knee in shock. That could have been it, our entire quest brought roundly to an end as a result of arrogance and greed, had it not been for a fierce punch from Percival on the young knight's greave, throwing him off balance and bringing him tumbling to the floor. Percival's wrath was unmeasurable, a bloodthirsty rage as he pinned his opponent and pounded fist after fist upon his delicate cheeks until his fair hair began to run red. The signal for submission was given, and the duel was over.

Percival snatched the Necklace from the Emperor's grasp, no words of gratitude or courtesy as he walked past his blood-soaked opponent. Gawain and I stood and offered our gratitude to Charlemagne, for whatever it was worth. We knew there would be no rest for us in his court that night, and mounted our horses without delay.

Writings of Sir Galahad – Day 42

Our pace across the north of Gaul was relentless. Percival never tired, despite strong protests from Gawain, who was still suffering from his sores. Our camps were brief. I caught a few hares and gathered some berries to keep Gawain's strength up, but he was becoming weaker by the day. However, upon reaching the shore and seeing our British Isles lying not more than a few miles away, it was as if a tonic had been administered to us all. We were so close to success.

Percival had bribed a local fisherman to take us across the stretch back to our homeland in exchange for five of the emperor's gold coins. Within hours we had arrived on the white sands of Britain once more. Relief rushed over us. Gawain and I prostrated ourselves and kissed the earth the moment we disembarked. Even Percival let out a bellowing scream in triumph and cursed the continental lands we had left behind. Word of our return spread quickly through the southern villages, and riders of our king met us at Fort Venta before escorting us back to Camelot.

There was much fanfare upon our return to our fabled stronghold, King Arthur himself rushing out from the castle gates ahead of his knights to embrace Sir Percival. Lady Guinevere was the first to acknowledge Gawain and me, relieved at our safe return, but a hint of resentment was etched across her face. This was swiftly countered by the smooth delights offered by Morgan le Fay, eager to hear of our travels. That evening, Camelot's walls were lit with flames in celebration of the retrieval of the Palladium, grandly presented by Percival himself in front of all eleven Knights of the Round Table, even earning applause from the usually restrained Sir Lancelot. The king declared the statue to hold the key to the future of Britain, and blessed his wife for her visions together with Morgan le Fay's counsel. Further rapture ensued when Percival also presented our king with the Necklace earned through combat in the court of Charlemagne. It glowed deep red like never before. It was Morgan le Fay who suggested this be a gift to Lady Guinevere, perhaps to comfort her for whatever grief she had experienced of late. King Arthur agreed and our lady was adorned with its alluring charm.

Cheers and trumpets sounded and *'All hail King Arthur and his Round Table'* echoed from every corner of Camelot's great hall. I felt at once a sense of wonder and discomfort, managing to bring my hands together for applause for all but a brief moment. I could not help but notice Gawain was the same. I caught his eye, he caught mine, we both caught Merlin's, his face sour and stern with the weight of the world upon him. Something was amiss.

Writings of Sir Galahad – Day 48

Not a week has passed since our wondrous return from our quest for the Palladium, the 'Grail' as Percival, Gawain and I have secretly called it up to now. The unease both I and Gawain have felt since our return to Camelot has not been shaken. Even as we lie with our wives at night we are brought out of slumber by strange visions of ancient warriors, wreathed in blue fire, screaming in anguish. We have tried to seek the counsel of Merlin, but alas, he is nowhere to be found, not seen since the evening of celebration upon our return.

Percival appears not to share our cursed nightmares, and neither Gawain nor I would consider him a liar. We have noticed though that his usual lust for life has dwindled, his interest in women seemingly extinguished. He lusts only for the Palladium, and agrees to stand watch over it for many a night, regularly coming into confrontation with Sir Lancelot, who also recently appears to be bewitched by its charm. It has not gone unnoticed at court that the king's most trusted companion Sir Lancelot has been spending more time with our Lady Guinevere, a poisonous affair not even worth tempting the mind should it come to pass. Whispers grow however among the Knights of the Round Table, which side we would choose should the king be betrayed. Those that remain loyal to the Pendragon family agree that King Arthur would and always will be the rightful ruler of Briton, and prepare to side with his Red Dragon banner until the end of days. Sir Lancelot though, has always been held in high esteem by the Round Table for his unrivalled skill in battle, and should he win the heart of our Lady Guinevere as well, the rift within the council I fear will be irreconcilable. What would such a split bring to our kingdom? Saxon rule? The raising of the White Dragon standard over Camelot? Never in my lifetime, I swore to Arthur. We all did – at least we thought so at the time.

Enough! I must rid myself of these incarnations of dread. The Round Table will never allow itself to be broken. Even when the time comes and our king passes over to the eternal shores of Avalon, we and our descendants will continue to serve the throne of Britain and pledge loyalty to his first child, Mordred.

We will serve.

CHAPTER 6

THE SINAI PENINSULA – EGYPT

2nd March 2012 AD

A S THE SOUNDS OF ADHAN CAME THROUGH THE WINDOWS WITH the evening light, Aisha opened the door of her father's study. She knew she had been warned not to enter, both by him and her mother Amal, who was busy downstairs cleaning, but her curiosity couldn't be suppressed.

Her father had not joined her or her mother in prayer for several days now, always citing work. His prayer mat lay in a corner of the room covered with dusty books and parchments, his desk littered with more of the same. Aisha coughed a little from the plume of spores released as she accidentally kicked over a tower of folders, trying to hold her breath so as not to draw attention. Her father had left immediately following his briefing from the woman she knew as Lady Morgan, and from what she had overheard, a trip to Mount Sinai was imminent for both her and her mother. No doubt her father would bodge some clumsy excuse as he always did to justify their trip – historical research, religious pilgrimage or whatever. Aisha's childhood had been far from normal, travelling from place to place at her father's whim, never settling down long enough to make friends or finish studies. Much of what she had learnt had come from her mother, and she chose her view of the world as opposed to the more myopic view of her father's teachings. Yes, she knew about the endless struggles between Islam and Christianity, as well as the Gaza Strip and the plight of the Palestinians. Her perspective was that each generation before her had failed to rectify the issues, and it was down to her generation to make amends, to learn from one another rather than repeat the mistakes of the past.

'Your father believes in the divine right of Allah,' her mother would say in reassurance. 'This is the work to which he is committed. Securing our rights and beliefs for you and your children.' This all sounded noble and just to Aisha when she was young, but one need only switch on a news channel to see where this attitude had left the leaders of most faiths. While the childhood stories her father told her had very much supported the teaching of the Koran, her mother would often bring up a more unique perspective, one of knights and lineage in the bloodline of Palamedes. Muddling matters was the concept of western crusaders joining with eastern Saracens under inhospitable circumstances in the Holy Lands of the 12th century. However, the idea that two key religions could put aside their differences and work together for a greater cause appealed to Aisha far more.

A few sketches and photographs were pinned up on her father's study walls. There was some pattern to them, but nothing Aisha could immediately work out. One of an ancient Greek statue, another of a necklace around the neck of Lady Morgan, although from the look of the clothes she was wearing, in a completely different era, possibly early Victorian. Then some more disturbing snippets of what looked like CCTV footage capturing grainy images of faces, mostly young to middle-aged men, British she would guess from the camera sources and scribbled captions below, suggesting locations from London to Edinburgh. One in particular depicted a man perhaps not much older than she, shot in Al-Khums, Libya about a year ago. Aisha couldn't make out the activity in the photograph, but it appeared to depict fire or flame, bright enough to cast a ring around the individual. She translated her father's notes below as simply 'Band', unsure exactly as to what this meant.

Curiosity still not satisfied, Aisha rummaged through more of her father's notes. She had heard from the earlier discussion with Lady Morgan the significance of the forthcoming lunar eclipse, so she was not surprised to see a book of astrology lying open on the side table, although she thought that astrology was not really a favourite hobby of her father's. What was beneath this book, however, drew her attention. A neatly bound series of parchments, all photocopied courtesy of a Mr Geraint South, in a language indecipherable by Aisha. The images, however, needed no explanation. A female figure garbed in green, her red hair flowing and eyes ablaze, surrounded by haunting black shadows swirling around her, the hands held high above her head to form a glowing golden triangle. the sun blotted out by the moon, and all the men and women depicted cowering and bowing with horror upon their faces. What sort of cursed world was this? And of what interest was it to her father? Aisha pulled out her mobile phone from her pocket and quickly took a photo, the click sounding just as the voice of her mother startled her from behind.

'You know not to come in here, child!' Amal growled from the doorway, hand beckoning her daughter out. 'If your father knew you were in here again he would have you whipped! Away with you now! Go!' she shouted. Aisha pouted for a moment before obeying with a huff and shoved past her mother in disgust.

'I take it Dad will not be joining us for prayers again this evening?' she retorted.

'We've been over this Aisha, your father is a busy man right now,' her mother defended, still shooing Aisha down the stairs.

'Too busy for prayer?' Aisha continued flippantly. Her response resulted in a firm clip round the ear from her mother.

'Do not question your father's loyalty to Allah young lady! You know better!' Amal cursed. 'He and his men have been defending our lands from foreign invaders for years, you know this! If it wasn't for him...'

'Foreign invaders like the West you mean? Like the very governments he is in contact with almost every day?' Aisha shot back harshly. Her mother fell silent. 'Face it, Mother. You know full well what he does, what he claims to have been doing these many years, is not for the sake of Islam. Or indeed any religion! Who exactly is Lady Morgan Worthington? Sir Lawrence Worthington? The White Dragon and the Red? Their ambitions don't appear in any passage of the Quran that I've ever been taught!' Aisha's face grew red with anger. Her mother seemed taken aback by just how much her teenage daughter had taken in secretly without her knowledge. She was no longer a little girl content with following orders, she was a young lady capable of making her own decisions. Amal hid a small smile from Aisha, casting a look down to the floor before walking past her towards the door.

'Come now... we'll be late for prayer.'

⁓୨୧⁓

Amal and Aisha walked slowly arm in arm towards their local mosque, politely offering a good evening to other families heading in the same direction. Aisha, still rattled, forced her pleasantries, then placed her hand on her mother's in solidarity.

'I'm sorry, Mother. You know I am. I appreciate how hard it has been for you to manage this whole situation – Father constantly being away, us moving from place to place.' Aisha spoke softly. Her mother gave a smile back, followed by a little chuckle.

'I forget sometimes just how old you know are, and how the world is forever changing. I love your father, deeply. I always will, but make no mistake... I want a better life for you, my child. I want you to learn as he has learnt, become aware of life's true challenges without the restraint of... well...'

'Being a woman?' Aisha finished with a laugh of her own.

'Your father is of a special bloodline as I'm sure you know. We call ourselves the Children of Palamedes – one of the Twelve.' Amal continued.

'The Twelve?' Aisha enquired.

'Twelve Knights. Knights of the Round Table – do you remember the stories I told you when you were very young?' her mother continued. Aisha did remember, but bedtime stories were not what she expected to hear about right now. The myths and legends from ancient Britain and King Arthur were well known of course... but were they connected to her and her family? Ludicrous.

'Sooo... are you telling me Father is a Knight of the Round Table? Does he fight dragons and ride stallions off into the sunset in exchange for the favours granted by fair maidens?' Aisha mocked in reply.

'All myths are grounded in some form of reality, Aisha. After all, look at all these people around you. Heading to pray to the heavens in thanks for all Allah has given us, just as Christians would to their God, Buddhists to theirs. However, how many of them do you think have actually *witnessed* any such deity? Just because something isn't apparent doesn't make it any the less important to us,' Amal proposed.

Aisha had to agree – legends can be embellished over the centuries by storytellers and folklore, in the same way as the miracles performed by gods and goddesses are first conceived. But the grain of inception had to come from somewhere, however human or indeed divine. Perhaps fairy tales of knights and maidens were not so far-fetched, and whatever their foundations may have been... they clearly had enough substance to preoccupy her father day and night.

'You said there were twelve? Twelve Knights?' Aisha enquired. 'What of the others? Does Father know them?'

Her mother fell silent once again as they approached the doors of the mosque. 'I believe he does... as you will need to do when the time comes.' She tidied the hijab around Aisha's forehead.

'Time? What time? Am I to become a knight?' Aisha couldn't resist breaking into a wide smile.

'You are of the bloodline, are you not?' her mother asked.

'But Father hasn't explained any of this to me! What am I supposed to do? Carry on whatever work he's been a part of all this time?' Aisha persisted.

Amal paused for a moment on the first step into the mosque. She turned and faced her daughter with a look that appeared both stern and fearful at once. 'I would recommend that you forge your own path when such a time comes. Decide for yourself that which is worth following and that which is not,' she whispered.

Aisha frowned at such a cryptic response. 'You…you don't approve of what Father's doing? Why? Is it because of his constant absence? The company he keeps?' she quizzed. Aisha was still mindful of several late-night arguments which had taken place at home between her mother and father, always assuming they were work-related, now perhaps given a different perspective. 'What about this?' Aisha showed her mother the photograph she had taken from her father's study, the figure in green and the blackened spirits surrounding it. Amal took her daughter's hand and led her to the side of the entrance.

'Your childhood friend, Bushra, do you still keep in touch?' came a prompt switch in topic from Amal.

'Yes, through social media. She's been living just outside London with her sister. Why?' Aisha replied.

'Perhaps it's worth paying her a visit? You can't have seen each other since you were very little?' her mother said, looking more distracted as she went on.

'Errr… no. Are you suggesting I should go to London? Now? What is this? Is it the photograph? I promise I won't pry into father's work anymore if it upsets you.' Aisha said with remorse. Her mother patted her hands in gratitude.

'Trust me, my dear daughter, I know. As I said though, you should have the right to forge your own destiny. That means understanding all the sides of an argument… like I've always taught you, remember?' Amal tried to smile through her seriousness.

Aisha took a deep breath then turned her gaze to her feet. 'If I go, you won't want me to seek out Lady Morgan or Sir Lawrence Worthington, will you?' she ventured. Her mother brought her palm up to her daughter's chin.

'Allen. Mr Richard Allen. I suggest you start there.'

CHAPTER 7

➤✦◆✦◀

ARTHURIAN BRITAIN

8th Century AD

'I DON'T RECALL YOU GIVING ME AN ANSWER, MERLIN.' MORGAN le Fay stubbornly stood beneath the stone arched doorway of the warlock's chambers in the northern tower of Camelot. Her eyes fixed on every move her mentor made as he paced up and down stroking his long, fine winter-white beard.

'Because I owe you none, Morgan!' Merlin eventually erupted, wagging his wrinkled finger in her direction. 'Your actions with the king... sending Sir Percival, Sir Galahad and Sir Gawain off in search of a fabled Greek treasure. You have no idea what you may have started!'

'And you do?' Morgan squared up to her superior. 'Foolish old man. Why didn't you interpret the dreams of Lady Guinevere as I did? You must have known of their meaning! The people of Greece and their gods and goddesses – Minerva, the one they call Pallas Athena in their tongue. The power to command an *empire*. It was foreseen. Don't try to deny it!' she spat.

Merlin turned his back and placed both hands on his slate stone table. 'Of course, I knew... and like you, I too foresaw the consequences of retrieving the item known as the Palladium. Texts going back centuries describe its power, from a time when magic was not necessarily confined to realms or people. When the spirits of the earth and heavens were one – true gods and goddesses as you say, not meaning to walk amongst us mortals, but purely guide… sometimes even taunt us like rats in a cage. Always remaining omnipotent,' he muttered.

'You're afraid of them, aren't you?' Morgan replied. 'The great Merlin, who wrought the formidable Excalibur from the soils and waters of my kin, fearful of ancient folklore. Most amusing,' she hissed.

'If you truly believe it to be folklore Morgan, why the interest? And why, might I add, did you suggest to King Arthur that the three knights pay their respects at the court of Charlemagne during their quest? He's hardly an ally of Britain,' Merlin questioned drily. Morgan fell silent, but gave a slight smile as she walked to the open window.

'This land you call Britain, and all those creatures that so many of its people have grown up believing in and revering. Spirits of the earth and water like you and I, soon to be drained of all our power in the face of a new world. A world of devoted followers of so-called 'gods,' created purely for power and control. Charlemagne and his followers of Christ follow this path, Merlin, they will bring it here like a plague, and we will be forgotten. Is that what you want? To see this cherished isle you and the Pendragon family have fought so hard for, fall into the hands of the enemy?' she said icily.

'How do you know who the enemy is, Morgan? You speak of two worlds – forever at war – yet forget the very principle of the Round Table and what its knights represent. Equality, honour, perseverance. One is not greater than the other… not even the king himself,' Merlin replied.

'Keep telling yourself that, Merlin, if it aids your rest at night.' Morgan turned back with a look of stone. 'Yet you know as well as I that mankind is *weak*… always seeking more than they have. Why else would your champion Arthur accept my proposal to search for the Palladium, the very artefact that helped create the Greek and

Roman Empires, and more? What is an empire if not to rule over others?' she argued.

'There was a reason the Roman Emperor Romulus Augustus returned the Palladium to its rightful place in Greece and the family of Thebes. He saw what it had done to his people. His empire had to fall. Had he had the sense to destroy the Necklace of Harmonia with it, then the future need not repeat the past.' Merlin's temper grew once more.

'But he *didn't* destroy the Necklace. What does that tell you of men? They will never be rid of greed and lust. You fight a war that cannot be won… but which can be controlled. Bent to our will!' Morgan flared with passion. Merlin cast his hands up in exasperation, seized a goblet and quaffed the berry wine. 'Don't ignore me, Merlin… you *know* I'm right.' Morgan continued to press.

'You said the wives of Sir Galahad and Sir Gawain are with child?' Merlin enquired pensively. Morgan nodded. 'It will not be their first and only son, having both drunk from the Well of Ares at Thebes… or Ares as the natives there would have said.' Merlin gave a slight belch as he thumbed through a pale leather-bound book. 'There was a group of warriors, born first from the Theban founder Cadmus, who initially drank from the well. Many of these sons grew up strong and fierce, potentially with powers of their own, according to the writings of Ptolemy of Alexandria, General to Alexander the Great. How powerful, I've never been able to determine for sure. He and Alexander were said to have slaughtered them down to the last man during the Battle of Chaeronea over eight hundred years ago. I did not witness it,' he muttered.

Morgan approached his shoulder and took a look at the book with her own eyes. 'So, one son will be born of this *warrior* bloodline… the other I assume will be the heir to their swords?' she speculated. Merlin closed the book with a shrug.

'The bloodline of Ares had a flaw however, given they cared not for the female, only the male. They fought side by side with their lover, as our knights would for their wives – which reminds me, what of Sir Percival? Has he settled with a maiden?' Merlin asked. Morgan gave a shake of her head before going on to explain his apparent obsession with the Necklace won in the duel with Charlemagne's champion. 'I told you... that Necklace will only bring about the downfall of the king and all that serve him. Don't think I haven't noticed Lady Guinevere and Sir Lancelot of late... such an affair, enchanted or otherwise, will be enough to split the Round Table in two,' Merlin cursed.

'Would that be such a bad thing?' Morgan posed. 'Arthur grows weak, his enemies stronger... perhaps it is time to seek an alternative to the throne of Britain? One that will ensure the kingdom's survival, together with its loyal followers.'

'Followers to you, you mean? You and your obsessions!' Merlin countered. 'Indeed, with the Palladium and the Necklace combined, Britain could lead the way in the destiny of this world's future. Or at least their holder could. All born of blood, of course.'

'Name me an empire that was not born of blood, Merlin,' Morgan challenged. 'I for one would rather keep my hands on the reins of the stallion than be in its path when it charges,' she smiled as she turned to leave.

'And what of Excalibur?' Merlin fired at her back. 'Do you truly believe Sir Lancelot, Prince Mordred or even you, spirit of the Earth and Stone, could control this most powerful relic? Bend it to *your will* as you say?' he said sternly. 'You may wish to speak with your sister of the lake... for that sword is not merely a weapon of destruction for anyone to wield. The king knows this, as does his most *loyal* of knights.'

Merlin's words of caution were enough to make Morgan pause momentarily. She turned. 'I'm sure there will always be those willing to *sacrifice* whenever necessary, Merlin,' she smiled, nodded in acknowledgement, then proceeded out of the chamber.

Merlin watched her lean frame, dressed in deepest green, slide out of view like a snake returning to the grasses. He curved the side of his mouth. 'Alas, my child, if only I could teach you exactly what *true* sacrifice was,' he whispered to himself.

CHAPTER 8

━━━◈◆◈━━━

CARDIFF, WALES

1st April 2012 AD

NICK BUTCHER SWUNG HIS STAFF WIDE ABOVE HIS HEAD, FULLY expecting Luke to block, but he didn't. Instead, the moderate blow landed squarely on Luke's upper arm, causing him to yelp and stagger backwards. That was the fourth time during the sparring session.

'Need to lift your guard,' Nick sniggered. 'You and I are the same height, no reason why you cannot shield such a move.'

Luke rubbed the sore spot, trying to hide his temper. He was tempted to make a derogatory comment about Nick Butcher's waistline, contrasting it with their equal height, but managed to refrain. He lifted the wooden staff of Excalibur in defence once again, noting that despite appearing more solid than those of other knights, it certainly didn't have the same length or reach.

'You do realise that most enemies I come across would just go for the pistol, right?' Luke quipped.

'Sure. Let's see how that little pop-gun of yours measures up against Lady Morgan and her powers. Or the blades of Larry or Geraint. No. If you are to have Excalibur, you're going to have to learn to wield it… properly,' Nick tailed off before lunging at Luke once again, this time Luke parrying well.

Adam and Violet sat quietly on one of the pub benches, spectating. Violet let out a little chuckle every time her father landed a blow on Luke.

'Well, your brother might have the looks of the family, but it's safe to say you've got the brawn,' she joked as Luke fell to the floor for the umpteenth time.

'You're enjoying this, aren't you,' Adam smiled. 'Your father's certainly quite the taskmaster.'

'Like Richard wasn't?' Violet pushed Adam gently. 'Anything my dad has picked up, it would have come from yours!'

The two continued to laugh until Adam caught sight of Gary and Mr Bishop trotting hurriedly out of The Blue Hare pub, Beth just behind holding a tray of drinks. Violet picked up on his concern.

'Have we gotten any further as to where Lady Morgan and the White Dragon might be going? Where they have taken the Palladium?' she asked. Adam shook his head. 'All Gary's contacts, Carl Bishop's research... surely there must be something?' she flustered. Adam continued to shake his head. 'You would have thought the White Dragon would have made a sound by now? Y'know, like they did last time with the invitation to the Imperial War Museum?' she thought out loud.

'They wanted to be found then,' Adam replied. 'And let's not forget that for many of these more recent encounters Lady Morgan and Sir Lawrence had a spy working for them.' His voice grew cold.

Violet scuffed her shoes on the pebbles beneath in an attempt to look distracted, despite clearly touching a sensitive nerve by mentioning Iain Donnelly. She decided Adam was brave enough to speak openly and needed no pity – it was not the Allen family way. 'Do you think you loved him? Iain I mean?' she asked bluntly. Adam turned, looking shocked at the direct nature of her question, but managed to respond immediately, surprising even himself.

'Yes. Yes, I believe I did.' Adam said without eye contact.

'Sorry. We don't have to...' Violet began.

'No, it's fine Violet. I know these past few months I've not been easy to live with. I suppose I thought I was doing both you and Luke a favour by sparing you my feelings. Truth is I was only sparing myself.

This is long overdue… but thank you.' Adam's little speech was heartfelt. 'When I was with Iain, either fighting by his side or just… well, in his company, I felt stronger. My father told me this would happen, but only when I had a partner, someone I cared about, like the Sacred Band warriors have always done. It's in the blood I guess.'

Violet resisted the urge to put a comforting hand on his shoulder. The time wasn't right. 'Luke said when you and Iain fought outside The Bear the day I was captured, something happened between the two of you… something powerful?' she queried. Adam gave an unsettling smile.

'Not sure exactly what that was. It all felt a little bit like a dream. Iain was in trouble, I could see it, I just ran and kissed him like it was the last time we would ever be together. Next thing we knew….' Adam attempted to describe it but words wouldn't come. Now Violet felt the time was right for comfort, her hand sliding over his.

'Yeah, I think you loved him – you big softy you!' she teased. 'Your Dad was right… it took that sort of power to do what you did, not really anything stronger in this world is there?'

Adam sometimes forgot that the little girl he once knew, who scurried behind the pub counter washing tankards and plates, was now becoming a young woman. A headstrong one at that. He expected no less from the line of Sir Bors, and when the time would come for Violet to pick up her father's sword, like Karen and the line of Sir Kay, she would be a formidable and loyal knight.

Her words triggered something in Adam's mind. Was there really no greater power in the world than love for another? It all sounded very coy when presented that way, but no doubt it was true. He wondered about Lady Morgan and her violent response to holding Excalibur… perhaps there was more to this than just a sacrifice or simple blood offering? He looked at his brother, once again lying on his back following a brutal takedown by Nick… had Luke figured it out? Would he figure it out? Was Mary right to tease him by presenting him with the sword? So many questions with such little time in which to answer.

'You know all the other Sacred Band fighters… the ones Graham

McCreedy found. Do you think they are all together? Partners or lovers, I mean?' Violet chimed in again.

'Don't know. Probably.' Adam shrugged. 'They certainly displayed a fair bit of skill that evening on Arthur's Seat. Doubt us lot would have seen Lady Morgan off without them.'

'And you said there was only ever 300 of them… anywhere in the world? That's 150 couples?' Violet posed.

'Correct. So I'm told anyway.'

'Jeez. Well, if you're going to find your special someone, you might have to look further than dating apps!' Violet laughed. Adam gave a modest smile. 'Do you think Graham knows all of them? Surely not?'

'Very much doubt it. If he does, they're certainly not answering his calls!' Adam mocked while pointing over to a strident Graham pacing up and down the patio, mobile glued to his ear as he ordered poor Fernando about and shooed away Beth's offering of beverages.

'That chap certainly needs to chill a bit,' Violet said disapprovingly. 'I get the urgency, but seriously…!'

Adam scraped his nails across the bench as Luke protested at one of Nick's lower blows, followed by a threat of knocking the old man's teeth down his throat if it were to be repeated. 'This might get ugly towards your dad in a minute,' he warned Violet.

'For which one?' Violet replied, settling back on the bench table, completely unfazed.

'Damn, I swear, Nick, if you hit me with that magic toothpick of yours one more time I'll….' Luke steamed.

'You'll what? What? Thump me? Let's see you try, son of Richard, son of Galahad, bearer of Excalibur! What that little lady-friend of yours was thinking, handing you the ultimate prize, was anyone's guess!' Nick roared back. Adam was taken aback by Butcher's ferocity, but noticed a marked change in Luke's behaviour upon hearing the reference to Mary Cassidy. A second or two of complete composure… then blind rage. Luke threw himself at Nick, short wooden staff in hand, battering wildly like a caged beast lashing out in all directions. No control. Or so it appeared.

Nick easily deflected the ill-tempered attack at first. Then, Luke's blows became stronger, still lacking in effectiveness, however. The wooden staff began to make an unnatural sound upon contact with Nick's, almost like the mild rumble of thunder upon impact. A huge uppercut in hand, with a bellow from Luke and a blinding moment of pure white light, and Nick's massive frame toppled a good two to three metres back. He groaned as he slammed into the short picket fence around the car park, bringing a section of it down. Violet rushed to his side in a panic. Adam leapt to his feet.

Luke was shivering, fruitlessly panting. Adam placed both his hands on his shoulders, urging him to settle. 'Breathe. Just breathe for a moment,' he reassured.

Nick was hauled back onto his feet, shaken, quickly trying to hide any discomfort or embarrassment in front of his daughter. 'What in the darkest hell was *that*?' he cursed.

'I'm... I'm sorry. I don't know.' Luke stuttered. 'It was as if I couldn't stop. I wasn't wielding this sword, the sword was wielding me!' he tried to explain while gasping for breath. Adam looked down at the wooden staff, now radiant as Excalibur itself, blade gleaming, hungry for more conflict. Then it quietly returned to its wooden form, mimicking Luke's own tapered aggression. Anger brought Excalibur out, but without the strength to control its emotions, it would relentlessly and remorselessly hack down everything in its path. A true harbinger of death, the end of all things. No wonder Mack Benson and the line of Bedivere needed to be so sound of mind in order to find it, let alone wield it, Adam thought.

'What made you stop?' Adam looked his brother squarely in the eye.

'Min. Minnie did.' Luke remained fixed on Nick and Violet, still weighed down with shame.

'She spoke to you?' Adam enquired.

'No, nothing like that. Not like when she appeared at the Forth Estuary either. It was me, I didn't... couldn't... betray her. Not after all she's... all she's....' Luke struggled.

'Sacrificed?' Adam finished. Luke swiftly turned, dropping

Excalibur to the floor and storming inside the pub without so much as a word. Adam bent down and picked up the wooden staff, examining it.

'Be careful, Adam,' Violet warned. 'You don't know what that thing might do.'

In fact, Adam was beginning to understand exactly what it might do, and to whom it would answer. His mind scrambled to explore each scenario to support his fledgeling theory. Karen's last words before she fell from the Imperial War Museum that night, William Wood throwing himself in front of Violet with Mack Benson there to witness it. A history of Bedivere descendants, at times of great strife, being able to source and summon Excalibur when it was most needed – not to wage war, but to end it. Choosing a higher path and comprehending its significance… what it was to sacrifice, and understand it. Not simply *witness* it – for that was not enough. Lady Morgan perhaps remained ignorant to this… after all, what had she ever loved more than herself? Not Sir Lawrence and all the other descendants of Lancelot during her extended life, that's for sure. Purely pawns of power for the followers of the White Dragon, to manoeuvre however she saw fit. Had the Necklace of Harmonia and all its corruption and greed poisoned her from the moment she possessed it? An endless cycle of power, connected through its counterpart, the Palladium.

All these blazing thoughts whirled through Adam's mind like fragments of a jigsaw, to the point of complete distraction, even when a taxi pulled up right outside The Blue Hare's entrance. Beth hurried over to inform the guest that the pub was closed until six o'clock, but this didn't deter the new arrival.

A young woman, dressed in tight jeans which emphasised her shape, and a top which exposed her bronzed midriff, walked confidently over to Adam. She shifted her weathered rucksack strap from one shoulder to another before asking, 'Excuse me. Do you know where I might find a Richard Allen? My name is Aisha. Aisha Hussin.'

CHAPTER 9

—◆◈◆—

ARTHURIAN BRITAIN

8th Century AD

'I HAVE BEEN DECEIVED!' THE KING ROARED, STUMBLING INTO THE hall of the Round Table, blood oozing between the plates of his armour. 'That roach! That weasel! Lancelot! He lies and betrays me!' he choked out before slumping into one of the thirteen evenly spaced chairs. His breathing became laboured as the wound started to take its toll, his eyes briefly rolling back then snapping lucidly forward once more. Two young pages dressed in loose red tunics hurried to his side to help remove the breastplates and free the king's chest, both looking at each other despondently upon revealing the full extent of his injuries.

'Percival. Where's Percival? Bring him before me... *now*.' The king rallied, the blade of Excalibur clanging down upon the table, still stained from its previous victim. One of the stewards ran off in a fluster at the request, the other tried to encourage a few sips of water. 'This... this is the result of disloyalty of the highest order. To lie in the bosom of my beloved Guinevere, to turn my own son against me, to take my knights! To spread ill will around court and poison the minds of my own kin – all to win the favour of the Saxons. The... the *swine,*' he choked once more, spilling the water, and shooing away the fussing steward.

The chamber door creaked open, a battered gauntlet curled itself around its edge. Sir Galahad staggered in, Sir Bedivere drooping off his shoulder, about ready to drop at any second. 'Sire. Are you hurt? I saw you fall from your horse just outside the main castle gates,' Galahad asked. The king winced slightly but did not answer.

'We are holding the walls for now. Sir Gaheris led a counterattack on the east wing but I've not heard of its outcome. Sir Bors is still deep in the affray with his men and Sir Kay, I fear, may have fallen to the Saxon flank on the west,' Galahad reported while helping Bedivere to his seat. 'We might be able to hold Camelot, but Sire, I would strongly advise you and Lady Guinevere to retreat to the haven of Glastonbury. From there, you can make swift passage across the moors back to Tintagel,' he continued to advise. The king proved obstinate.

'I travel nowhere with Guinevere. Let Lancelot take the harlot! The two have been plotting this for many a moon now. No, Sir Galahad, I shall not flee my own home and stronghold only to give that Saxon horde the satisfaction of witnessing my retreat. I shall *stay,*' the king wheezed. Galahad stared for a moment before bowing in acquiescence. He quietly took the seat next to his king, running a finger along the pommel of Excalibur.

'Arthur, you know we cannot allow Mordred to take this. Think of what it could do in the hands of such an unhinged mind. With Morgan le Fay also by his side, your son and Sir Lancelot could form an alliance capable of overthrowing the mightiest of monarchs. Even *you.*' Galahad sighed. Just the thought of such treachery being spoken of in this hall was enough to bring the king to his feet and seize Excalibur with both his hands.

'The sword answers to me. Only *me.* Merlin promised me as much. Let that gnat of a witch try and take it from me... let her feel the full heft of its power over her paltry tricks. Morgan le Fay will soon come to learn that kings, and *only kings*, wield this sword!' Arthur bellowed, the outburst sapping his strength with every word, his ageing body failing and bringing him back to his seat. Galahad had seen more and more of these maniacal outbursts from his king of late, ever since he and his two fellow knights Percival and Gawain had returned with the Palladium. A similar sickness had overcome Percival, as if the great knight was wrestling with inner demons none could comprehend. All interest in food, wine and women evaporated, as he sought only the satin-smooth words of a local Christian pastor for aid, a move that had enraged his king along with several of his own men. Whatever this newfound god was that Emperor Charlemagne and his Pope so warmly preached, Sir Percival appeared to have found some measure of solace from it.

'Mordred is of *your* blood, Arthur,' Galahad whispered. 'Would it not stand to reason that he too could wield this blade? Just as we knights pass down our own swords through the generations?'

King Arthur pondered this for a moment, then quickly turned the tables and asked, 'Are your wife and your two sons safe?' Galahad cocked his head to one side quizzically.

'How did you know I had two sons?' he asked.

'Merlin, he told me you would. Sir Gawain can expect the same I hear – whether both held in the womb at once or as night follows day, you shall have two sons, he said,' Arthur replied.

'He was certain?'

'As only Merlin can be. Your quest across the far continent and the land of the Greeks. The city of Thebes where you found that cursed statue… there was a well there, yes?' Arthur strained through a surge in the pain.

Galahad tried to recall. The thirst both he and Sir Gawain felt when entering the Theban Temple, which they slaked from the well before they found the Palladium… perhaps untouched for centuries. The vivid dreams the two had shortly after, the cries of wounded soldiers perishing upon the battlefield, arm in arm sometimes. The two would occasionally talk of it, but rarely hazard a guess about their occurrence. All they knew was that Sir Percival appeared unaffected, but then he had not drunk from the well.

'What else did Merlin tell you?' Galahad enquired. 'Did he predict any of this? The Palladium and its powers? Are they real?'

Arthur shifted uneasily in his seat. 'A great empire, Morgan le Fay said. Like Rome and Greece before us. Unrivalled in its reach and influence. Why Merlin did not tell me is a riddle. She told me he was a traitor, he wanted such power for himself. Merlin on the other hand warned me of such dangers, bringing ancient relics to these shores… both tokens should have been left well alone.'

'Both?' Galahad questioned. 'The Necklace?'

'Indeed – Merlin spoke of both. An apparent connection between the two. What one appears to grant, the other can take away or corrupt. It's what befell the empires of Greece and Rome, maybe others. An endless circle, he called it, of love and desire, passion and deceit.' Arthur's tone became mournful. He scanned the Thirteen seats before him, six remaining loyal, the other six disloyal and vengeful. A brotherhood of equals torn apart. Was this to be his legacy? A Britain divided?

Sir Bedivere began to come to, groaned a little before wiping the dirt from his eyes. Galahad came to his aid and tended to the oozing head wound with some cloth. 'Where is the Necklace now?' Galahad asked. 'Is it still with Lady Guinevere?'

Arthur grunted a yes. It all started to make sense to Galahad. Why Morgan le Fay first raised the prospect of obtaining both the Palladium and the Necklace during their quest, perhaps knowing the Emperor Charlemagne would have the latter in his possession after the fall of Rome. It would explain his own aspirations for the Palladium, and equally, Sir Percival's renewed drive to obtain the Necklace in the duel. With both objects in the hands of Morgan le Fay, she could control both the peak and trough of the tides, winning countless others over to her cause. Perhaps, just as the Necklace tempted men when it was adorned, the king's wife Guinevere, maintaining both beauty and youth, Morgan le Fay could combine it with her magic and rule for eternity. A faithful Sir Lancelot and five other knights, Lamorak, Geraint, Palamedes, Gareth, Tristan and all their progeny, remained by her side. The very thought chilled Galahad to his core.

No. He and his sons would take a stand, as would all the children of the Round Table still loyal to the once and future King of Britain, commander of Excalibur and the standard of the Red Dragon, in the face of its white Saxon counterpart. If eternity is what it took, then for eternity he would stand.

The steward sent off to find Sir Percival returned with flushed cheeks and in a sweat, unable to complete his task. He did, however, present the pale robed figure of Merlin, dishevelled and unshaven, skin sagging around the jaw and neck. He leaned on his thorn staff and bowed as always to the king. Arthur beckoned him over and leaned in close for his whispered advice, eyes narrowing then widening as he absorbed what Merlin said. 'Are you mad, Druid? This surely cannot be the way?' the king blurted out loud. Merlin backed off, head still bowed low in subjugation.

'What? What are we to do, Sire?' Galahad asked. The king gripped the Round Table to pull himself up to his feet.

'Sir Bedivere, I shall have need of you once this is done. Sir Galahad, return to your wife and children. No more service can be done here in Camelot, you are to accompany Merlin to Glastonbury,' Arthur commanded.

Aghast, Galahad began to protest, but one stern look from Merlin and he withdrew. His wife Elaine was safe just outside the city walls, away from the carnage, along with his two sons. Although every ounce of him longed to be with them, to clasp them safely to his chest, the thought of abandoning his king troubled his heart. Was there no other way?

'I ask this of you, Sir Galahad. You are to keep my banner flying, the Red Dragon, in defence of this sword, Excalibur, and when the Kingdom of Britain is most in need, it shall return,' Arthur predicted, hand placed firmly on Galahad's shoulder.

'Surely, Sire, with Sir Bedivere in his current state, I should accompany you?' Galahad proposed.

'No. Away with you. Go with Merlin and your wife and children – I have spoken. Sir Bedivere, you come with me.' The king stumbled forward, Bedivere sucking in deep breaths to join him by his side as the two headed for the intricately carved door, the chaos of battle echoing in the distance as it opened. 'In all our lifetimes, we must make a sacrifice for love, Sir Galahad, this one shall be mine. Yours and Bedivere's shall come. This I promise you,' were Arthur's final words as he disappeared, Excalibur's blade shining as brightly as ever. Bedivere bowed dutifully to Galahad as he followed the king.

A crisp winter breeze caught Galahad's face as he rode steadily by Merlin's side. He dared not look back at Camelot and the piercing cries as men slaughtered men... some who until recently would have called each other family. His stomach churned at the thought of abandoning his post in such a fashion. He should be there, by Arthur's side to the end. His grip on the reins tightened in agitation, only Merlin's soothing words restraining him.

'Merlin, I cannot stand for this. We swore an oath upon these very swords you made for us out of sacred thorn tree, to protect the king and his realm. Why are you forcing me to flee?' Galahad disputed. Merlin was never one for conversation, and remained fervently focused on the dusty track ahead for some time before reciting:

'Those that know love, but feel its true pain,
Shall watch their empire be born once again.
Those that are cursed, but destined to lead,
Will first taste desire, followed by greed.
So goes the circle, the rise and the fall,
Spare the blade of the king, by whose hand loses all.'

Galahad really wasn't in the mood for riddles, and pushed for more answers, although he did reflect on Merlin's words in his head. Lady Guinevere's dreams were interpreted as a form of loss and grieving by Lady Morgan, he was told, perhaps a true love that brought about an empire – the source of the Palladium. Sir Percival's actions upon their return from the continent and subsequent actions would reflect a form of desire and greed, as would that of Sir Lancelot towards the king's wife, both of whom had never been the same since the arrival of the Palladium and the Necklace.

The 'blade of the king'… this had to be Excalibur. But the 'losing all' at its hand, was this the sacrifice of which Arthur spoke? The king had, of course, wielded the majestic blade on several occasions in the face of his enemies, but never under such precarious circumstances. 'Will King Arthur and Sir Bedivere die?' Galahad asked Merlin.

'Arthur, yes. Not Bedivere,' Merlin responded bluntly.

'How are you so sure?'

'Because Sir Bedivere will not be fighting, not at least until the king is dead, along with his son.'

'Mordred? He won't get Excalibur?'

'Not his destiny. No.'

Then what is? Galahad thought, not wanting to embarrass himself by asking the great druid what could be perceived as a feeble and naïve question. Mordred surely posed the greatest threat, alongside Morgan le Fay, especially should Excalibur fall into his hands, a new King of Britons, no more than a puppet with Morgan le Fay wielding the strings. A pulse of milky-white light shot across the sky, and Galahad turned back towards Camelot fearing the worst.

'What was that? Merlin? Answer me, old man!' Galahad spat.

Merlin scanned the horizon, listened to the return of bird song and the drowning out of human cries, a smile stretched across his wrinkled face. 'As I said, not in Mordred's destiny.'

'The king has killed his own *son?*' Galahad flustered.

'No.'

'So Mordred and his men have killed Arthur then? Which is it?'

'The king and his son have killed each other. But it is Arthur who has sacrificed with love in his heart for *more* than just himself. The lesson has been learnt by the king, sadly not by his son Mordred… nor indeed Morgan le Fay,' Merlin said with a satisfied grin.

'How can you be so sure?' Galahad pressed.

'The battle is over. The war, however, has only just begun,' Merlin hinted, putting a distance between his horse and Galahad's. 'Come, keep up, Sir Galahad,' he chuckled. Galahad muttered out a curse under his breath and followed.

'So, what happens now? Sir Bedivere has Excalibur? Was that your plan?' Galahad asked. Merlin's expression gave him his answer. 'Where's he going to take it?'

'It will go with the king. His body will travel far north from here – don't worry, young knight, Nimue will guide him,' Merlin reassured.

Galahad had heard this name before – *Nimue* – the spirit of the lake. Both he and Morgan le Fay had been known to speak of such spirits buried deep within the earth of the kingdom, pre-dating perhaps the lands themselves. As time passed, such legends were becoming feeble fantasies, which were likely to disperse further over time, like the winds that carried them.

A welcome sight came into view. Galahad spotted his wife Elaine and their two young boys sitting huddled beneath an oak tree, the evening rain dripping through its leaves. He leapt off his horse and rushed over to them, wrapping his arms around all three tightly before claiming a deep kiss. Moments later, Sir Gawain appeared, with his pregnant wife and young daughter on his saddle, having received the same advice from one of Merlin's ravens as the messenger. The group waited as the mists of the moors obscured the low fires still burning around the edges of Camelot. Then emerged the solitary figures of Sir Bors, Sir Gaheris and Sir Kay. Tears fell, then were wiped away as they regaled each other with their experiences and King Arthur's last stand against Mordred, the fatal blow permitted by the father only after he had taken a blade from one of his own men to defend his son in the bitter civil war. All witnessed, unchallenged, by a stoic Sir Bedivere. Poetic didn't begin to do the scene justice. Sir Percival was last seen kneeling before a cross of wood and wire as Sir Lancelot's men descended upon him.

CHAPTER 10

——————◆◆◆——————

CARDIFF, WALES

1st April 2012 AD

A N OLD, CRACKED GLOBE WAS PLACED IN THE CENTRE OF THE table by Beth. Aisha Hussin ran her index finger across it, then tapped lightly on a specific location. 'Here,' she said, 'that's where my father is, or at least where he said he was going.'

Adam leaned over and squinted his eyes. 'Egypt? Why Egypt?'

'I'm not sure, although he and the ghoulish lady on the screen were talking about Mount Sinai. Some sort of cultural significance?' Aisha replied.

'*Ghoulish lady*' Adam thought. Could only be one person. Aisha introducing herself as a Hussin all but confirmed his suspicions. Whether she could be trusted was all that remained to be seen now. 'Did your father tell you anything else?' he asked, keeping things deliberately vague.

'Only to stay put and not meddle,' Aisha returned with a cheeky grin. 'I believe he said the same to my mother, who, however, clearly thought otherwise.' Carl Bishop held a look of concern as he quietly stood up from his chair and riffled through the various files and folders on a separate table. He muttered softly to himself, the others only making out the occasional word.

'So, did your dad tell you anything about knights and swords?' Luke asked bluntly before Adam could silence him with a fierce glare.

'Actually, my mother did, yes. I can't confess to fully understanding, though. Something to do with our family bloodline? There are others... twelve I was told... and perhaps your father, Richard Allen, could assist me?' Aisha looked down as if puzzled by her own words. 'Could all be just nonsense.'

'It's not,' Gary reassured. 'Meet your fellow bloodlines.' He let out a sigh while gesturing to Luke, Adam, Nick and Violet. Aisha didn't know how to react so she kept a blank expression.

'Not sure I understand, Mr Willis. Sorry,' she replied. Gary went on to the abridged version of the Round Table, the Twelve Knights that remained subject to King Arthur, the loss of the thirteenth member Sir Percival as virgin, their differences forming the Red and White Dragon factions and their ambitions over these many centuries. Aisha absorbed what she could.

'We're all knights? All of us? From separate bloodlines but all from the Round Table?' she asked relentlessly.

'He's not. He's of the Sacred Band,' Luke again casually quipped, pointing to his brother. Aisha's eyes caught Adam's.

'Sacred Band?' she queried.

'From the Ancient Greeks of Thebes, yes. They were warriors, endowed with strength and power by the gods and goddesses of the time. They guarded the statue known as the Palladium, forger of empires. Your father Mr Hussin was looking for it in Libya last year, on behalf of his associates.' Adam hurried on. 'That's where I first met him.' He rolled up his sleeve to expose the thin scar line on his upper arm.

'My father did that? I'm... I'm...' Aisha tried to console him, but stalled. 'You said Sacred Band of Thebes? As in the tribe of Greece? They were all... weren't they? Are you...?' she tripped.

'Homosexual. Yes. As will be any one of the other three hundred that should form the Band at any one time. Some in relationships, some yet to find their soul mates.' Adam cut quickly to the point. 'We appear to draw closer to the bloodline of Sir Galahad and Sir Gawain, like my father and his close friend William Wood. But not sure that's exclusive, we've never been entirely...' Adam was interrupted by Aisha's switch in topic.

'Richard Allen, the man my mother mentioned. She said he could help. Is your father here?' she asked. Her audience turned silent.

'No, not anymore. Sorry.' Gary broke the tension.

'What happened?' Aisha looked concerned.

'The White Dragon killed him. Along with William Wood and several others, just a few months ago in Edinburgh,' Nick grunted, tightly folding his arms. The colour drained from Aisha's face. Her father was, as she feared, potentially involved in a murder. She was now sitting with those wanting revenge. She gripped the edges of her chair, not knowing whether to cut and run or try to justify. Gary decided for her.

'Please don't be afraid, Aisha. I know it's a lot to take in. None of us is suggesting you knew any of this, your father's activities and those of the White Dragon. But, you might be able to help us now that you are here,' Gary sympathised.

'Help *you*?' Aisha thought. I had come to seek their help, now they wanted mine? She settled a little after hearing Gary's words, although not enough to feel truly comfortable. She picked up her phone and swiped through her recent photos. 'Does this mean anything to you all?' she shared the image of the Lady in Green, the shadows and the lunar and solar eclipse. Gary took the phone, studied the photos a little before beckoning Carl over with urgency.

Violet invited Aisha to stay a few nights at The Blue Hare, Beth nodding in welcome despite Nick's obvious dislike of the idea. She drew the grumbling, heavy-set frame of Mr Butcher away to help make up one of the guest rooms while giving a wink to his daughter. Carl had darted back and forth between Aisha's phone and his papers, then focused on just one, a photocopy of an old Celtic manuscript. The likeness in the image was unmistakable.

'The transit of Venus, possibly,' Carl announced. 'A particularly holy event for many an ancient people, from Babylonian to Mayan. Symbolic of the feminine triumphing over the masculine. Could be the conjunction a mythical sorceress like Lady Morgan would look for.'

'Lady Morgan's a *sorceress*?' Aisha's question drew no response.

'When does it take place?' Adam queried.

'Fourth June,' Carl checked online.

'And the significance of Mount Sinai?' Gary pushed.

'Unsure. But its connections to Christianity, Moses and the Ten Commandments of the Bible might all play a part.' Carl gave a tired shrug.

'It's important to Islam as well,' Aisha chimed in. 'Mohammed and his journey to the heavens.' Adam became locked in thought. *Three* religions when Judaism is included, all contrary to Lady Morgan and her beliefs, now potentially at the mercy of her powers. Possibly more. The words of Iain rattled in his head once again... the more atheistic tone he had adopted during their final moments together in Arthur's tomb. A chance to seek revenge on anyone or any belief that had hurt him and those like them. Is this really what Lady Morgan had promised him? Promised all of the White Dragon followers? He snapped back into the room upon hearing Carl describe the image of the Lady in Green as a form of necromancy – a raising of the dead. Suggesting such an event could do far more than any superficial war or humanitarian conflict created in search of an empire. This was what Richard had always feared from the White Dragon, an event like no other. A final and merciless scourge of all those who had failed to show allegiance to the power of Morgan le Fay over these many centuries, perhaps in favour of other gods and goddesses. The faithful ones to be brought back from the shadows once more. One unique new world empire.

'She'll have both the Palladium and the Necklace of Harmonia ready to wield once the time comes,' Gary confirmed. 'And if she gets Excalibur?'

'Nothing can stop her,' Violet concluded.

Aisha leaned forward eagerly. 'Wait. There's an Excalibur? An actual Excalibur?' she pulsed with excitement. 'Where?' Luke lifted the smooth wooden token he had been holding tight in his hand since her arrival and waved it in front of her.

'Don't worry. I'll bring you up to speed,' Luke promised.

CHAPTER 11

⸺◈⸺

ALEXANDRIA – EGYPT

4th April 2012 AD

SWEAT HAD ALREADY BEGUN TO SOAK THE BACK OF SIR LAWRENCE'S crisp white shirt, the midday sun was so bright that it caused him to squint as he looked across the hazy harbour, cool mint tea in hand. Just under a week he'd been staying at his hotel by the Mediterranean coast, presented as official UK Government business of course, heading into the Egyptian general elections in only a few weeks, the allegiance of the Red Sea states being of the utmost importance. Truth was, he didn't care. Although his presence would be required back at Whitehall imminently, he had already prepared a waffling report, churned out in a few hours to satisfy ministers, met a few dignitaries and cordially shaken hands for the press. No more was needed. This had all become routine after so many years.

What was of more concern was the lack of focus from his wife of late. Lady Morgan was almost deliberately obtuse in answering his questions about the forthcoming transit of Venus and any necessary protocol. He was effectively a lackey, taking and relaying orders on behalf of the White Dragon, as opposed to the more familiar position of giving them. This new position did not sit well with him. He had comforted himself over these past months with blind faith in Morgan's abilities and beliefs – she had gotten him this far, lest he forget – with any momentary lapse in commitment quickly quashed by Geraint South and his academic rhetoric. He toyed with his wooden staff, the slim cane clicking neatly at the top, one sword within another, unique to the family of Sir Lancelot. He wondered whether his ancestors had ever doubted the great sorceress Morgan le Fay, her life extended by the Necklace of Harmonia, a well of wisdom and knowledge, surely unrivalled. That considered, he was not destined for immortality, he was no god, nor were his predecessors. Unlike Morgan, he had only one chance to get things right, not an unlimited series of second chances. A heavy sigh punctuated his thoughts as the hotel phone rang.

'Yes? Ah. Thank you, I was indeed expecting Mr South. He's in the lobby? I will be right down,' Sir Lawrence uttered while straining to interpret the accent on the other end of the line. A wipe of his forehead and straightening of his tie in the mirror shored up his confidence a little before he headed downstairs.

Across the ebony marble floor sat Geraint South, the sun-scorched skin on his usually pale legs looking out of place in the hotel. He waved his straw hat close to his face in frustration at the heat before clocking Sir Lawrence and raising a hand for attention.

'Sir Lawrence – sorry I'm a little late. Afternoon traffic in Alexandria is... well, the same as traffic anytime in this city!' Geraint chirped.

'Indeed. What have you to report?' Sir Lawrence cut directly to the point. 'Please don't tell me my near week-long stay in this furnace has been for little more than scouting the terrain. We have satellites for that!' his tone darkened.

'No, no. Sir, I can assure you everything has been necessary, absolutely necessary. Our lady was most insistent that I search the great library of Alexandria for all the texts that had a reference to the transit of Venus... anything that mentioned its significance in pagan mythology. Alexandria is one of the few libraries in the world that would hold such an ancient text,' Geraint gushed.

Sir Lawrence looked impatient. 'And?'

'Well, aside from a similar depiction of the Lady in Green which I know you've seen,' Geraint started to fluster as he produced the recorded picture already shared with Mr Hussin, 'I've found some fascinating detail concerning Lady Hypatia, a Greek woman, a mathematician and astronomer.'

'Hypatia?' Sir Lawrence queried.

'Yes, although the Christian texts would know her as Saint Catherine. As in the Catherine wheel? A fabled tale of the martyr condemned to death by Roman Emperor Maximian and the then Patriarch of this very city, Cyril of Alexandria, sometime in the fourth century and...'

'I am aware, Geraint. No lessons in how we got specific fireworks please,' Sir Lawrence quipped while wiping his forehead once more and ordering another mint tea.

'Apologies. Yes, of course. So, Lady Morgan considered Hypatia to be quite the inspiration it would appear, a model student of the cult of paganism. Her tireless work on the occult and astronomy led to many a fierce confrontation with those of Christian faith, even to an argument over when Easter should fall annually.' Geraint recomposed himself, producing another photocopy of a parchment. 'All a bit of speculation, but having studied what I can, it would seem as though Hypatia's challenge of what she saw as an undermining of pagan worship led her to drastic measures.'

Sir Lawrence leaned over the copy of the parchment with renewed interest. 'Did Hypatia hold the Palladium?' he asked.

'Unsure. But she almost certainly was aware of its potential through her family's teachings. In the face of severe persecution and the rise of the Roman Empire, would it not be rational to try and turn the tide in your favour by converting to an alternative faith?' Geraint continued. 'It is more than likely she held the Necklace of Harmonia, given her growing power and influence at a time of male dominance.'

Sir Lawrence murmured an acknowledgement, then caught another photocopied image in Geraint's hand. 'What's that?'

'This? Ah, this is interesting. It's a copy of one of the earliest astrolabes, an invention of Hypatia's according to some scholars.' Geraint smiled with excitement.

'The position of the planets?' Sir Lawrence confirmed.

'Indeed. So, why would a pagan take such an interest in the precise mathematical location of the planets?' Geraint proposed.

'For the transit of one in particular,' Sir Lawrence concluded. Geraint maintained his giddy smile. 'She was set to perform the ritual. Albeit with one important piece missing – *Excalibur.*'

'On what we now call Easter, correct. It would have served as a statement to all followers of the new religion that the Old Ways will never be gone, and their empire shall remain, always,' came the profound words of Mr South as he placed the copies down on the table, causing the glass of mint tea to shake.

Precise positioning, Sir Lawrence thought to himself. Knowing that Mount Sinai was of religious significance was not the full purpose of Lady Morgan's interest. In order for such a ritual to work, they needed to be in *exactly* the right location on the fourth of June, at the time of the transit of Venus. Although his wife had sensed it, she and the White Dragon would need to do more than be in or around the general vicinity when the time came. Still, with Mr Hussin's resources flooding into the desert peninsula as they spoke, together with firm foundations diplomatically, he felt confident in securing the objective. They still had two months.

'They even gave pilgrims to the site a silver ring, look.' Geraint fussed through yet more paper copies he'd found.

'Pilgrims? To where?' Sir Lawrence snapped back from his reverie.

'Why, to the monastery of Saint Catherine at the foot of Mount Sinai,' Geraint replied. 'Served as a bit of inspiration to loyal followers of the White Dragon most likely,' he continued, twisting his own embossed silver ring around his finger - *'Albus Draco,'* he smiled. Sir Lawrence gave an unsettled grin back.

A buzz came from the pocket of Sir Lawrence. He stood to pull out his mobile with a sweaty hand, fumbling over its buttons. A single, grainy image had been sent by Mr Hussin, courtesy of London Heathrow Airport and hacked CCTV footage. Sir Lawrence narrowed his eyes to try and make out the young female passing through customs, then read the accompanying message:

'My daughter, Aisha Hussin, sighted in England last week. Last known whereabouts, Cardiff. Action required immediately. Mr Hussin.'

'The naivety of youth indeed,' Sir Lawrence said to himself with a smile.

CHAPTER 12

CARDIFF – WALES

4th April 2012 AD

THE COARSE PENCIL SCRATCHED ACROSS GRAHAM MCCREEDY'S notepad – another voice message left. Another missed opportunity, he thought. In today's age of technology, the idea of simply calling those he once knew to check their whereabouts and whether they were busy seemed like an anachronism. He'd heard Adam and Luke joke about there being a mobile phone app of some sort for Sacred Band warriors across the world. Having spent the best part of three days relentlessly jotting down notes and punching in telephone numbers, such a method of keeping in touch would certainly have been more productive. Graham stretched his arms high above his head, releasing the tension in his chest, his weathered joints making clicking noises.

'How many?' Fernando asked while placing a glass of water in front of him.

'Not enough,' Graham sighed. 'Not that I could really expect much more. Most of those I knew have long since changed contact details, maybe even left the country. Very difficult to keep track.' He gulped some water, his throat dry from one-sided conversations with answering machines.

'Those that respond... can they share?' Fernando enquired. Graham shrugged. 'But, it's vital that they do, yes?'

'It is. You have to remember though many are now old, like me. They consider their best years behind them, and certainly don't wish to take part in any more wars. Even one of such significance. They have families to consider,' Graham replied despondently.

'Families? But Mr McCreedy, this could mean the end of such families, no?' Fernando protested.

'Everything comes to an end, my boy. Everything. The Sacred Band know this only too well.'

Fernando was unconvinced by Graham's casual answer. How could a select group of fighters capitulate so willingly in the face of such a threat? Yes, some were old, but so was McCreedy. Surely many would be like Adam Allen, mid-twenties and prepared to risk everything... especially if in a unique partnership with another Band member. Still, he had to process his own immaturity on the whole subject – just because he was now aware of this juggernaut of a situation didn't mean all those born into the Sacred Band would, many not having the same guidance the Allen family did through Richard and his closest allies. Despite the bond between the bloodlines of Sir Galahad and Sir Gawain, over the centuries various siblings would have undoubtedly gone unnoticed. Scattered across every continent, it was incredible that the descendants of the Round Table had managed to remain connected through the Red and White Dragon factions after so long. Graham often dubbed this 'the miracle of Merlin'.

The kitchen door flung open as Luke stomped his way in and slumped into the nearest chair, forehead oozing fresh blood. He tossed the staff of Excalibur clumsily onto the table and muttered a few curse words under his breath, Fernando and Graham only picking up a reference to Nick.

'Training going well, Master Allen?' Graham flippantly remarked. Luke's scowl silenced him. Beth knew the drill by now, soaked a tea towel in warm water and offered it to Luke to soothe his wound.

'He's getting better,' Adam encouraged, entering the room with Violet and Nick Butcher.

'Not quick enough though,' Nick grumbled. 'Two months we have, *two months*,' he reinforced with two raised fingers.

'Look, I smacked you on your ass before with this thing and I can do it again!' Luke flashed back.

'But you haven't. You haven't come close despite all your little tantrums and whining. If Morgan gets so much as a hand on that sword…' Nick paused to take a breath. Luke took his cue to leave before his temper got the better of him, grunting as he passed Aisha in the doorway.

'Still no Excalibur?' Aisha asked Violet.

'Not like before, the day you arrived. But he's getting good at taking punches,' Violet allowed herself to let out a small giggle.

Adam took the seat next to Graham. 'The Band? Have you managed to reach anyone else?' he quizzed. Graham passed his tatty notebook over.

'I'm out, I'm afraid, young Master Allen. About thirty replies, most not in relationships. Some even younger than you. Others, well, make me look fresh-faced.' Graham forced a smile. Adam scanned the list of scratched out names and ticks.

'You know all these people?' he asked.

'Most. Some vicariously, old acquaintances and such. Kids that have come out and since displayed powers that would fit the mould so to speak,' Graham replied.

'Can they all be trusted?' Adam calmly questioned. Graham picked up on his concern immediately, responding with a simple *yes*. Truth was, Graham could never be sure, and after Iain Donnelly – granted a name he'd never come across – anything was possible. Morgan and Lawrence Worthington's influence was spreading far deeper than most in the Red Dragon would ever have realised. It was a risk they'd have to take.

A buzz came from Aisha's pocket. It was her friend Bushra. Within moments of answering her face froze, her eyes squeezed shut as she tried to process the voice on the other end. A panicked jumble of words, tears and sharp breaths. It was Bushra, but something was very wrong.

'What? Who's been following you? Bushra, please try to calm down. What's going on?' Aisha composed herself. The call was cut off. 'Bushra? Bushra!' Aisha frantically tried to redial.

The group exchanged concerned looks. 'What's happened?' Violet asked. 'Bushra, your friend? She OK?' Aisha clamped a hand to her mouth, eyes still closed. The phone rang again, she answered immediately, but the voice was not Bushra's this time. A chilling, glottal tone with a heavy Middle Eastern accent. No one that Aisha recognised.

'Who are you? What have you done with Bushra?' Aisha demanded. Adam stood to attention by her side and gestured for the phone to be put on speaker.

'A daughter of Palamedes should really know better, Miss Hussin,' the voice rasped. Bushra's screams could be heard faintly in the background.

'Please. Whoever you are, if you're working for my father, this has nothing to do with Bushra. Let her go!' Aisha commanded. There was a painful silence.

'It has everything to do with her. No one is exempt, Miss Hussin. *No one*. You and your mother have made your allegiances known to the White Dragon. Most unfortunate that others less well versed than you and the Red Dragon on the actions to come, the glory that will be the new world, now need to suffer without comprehending exactly what they could have been a part of,' the voice taunted. Adam picked up a final few words spoken in Arabic before the stranger ended the call with '*Albus Draco*.' Aisha screamed Bushra's name into the static on the phone. Adam held her hands gently while attempting to draw out what information he could.

'Aisha, that voice. Did you know it? Was it your father?' he questioned. Aisha shook her head tearfully. 'Then who?'

'I don't know. My father knew many people, some simply guns for hire. I don't know. They could have killed her, they could have killed my mother...' Aisha flapped hysterically.

'He said something in Arabic, before *Albus Draco,* what did it mean?' Adam pushed.

'We… are… *watching.*' Aisha croaked.

Adam turned to the room of pale faces. 'Get Gary and Mr Bishop. We need to leave Cardiff right away.'

CHAPTER 13

———⊱◈⊰———

CARDIFF — WALES
4th April 2012 AD

'WE HAVE THREE CARS. FOUR IF YOU INCLUDE CARL'S,' GARY
said hastily. 'Nick and I can go in mine. Luke, take Aisha
and Violet. Adam, go with them. Graham and Fernando, stick together
and head back north to Scotland.'

'Violet is coming with me,' Nick snorted. 'And Beth….'

'I'm staying put,' Beth interrupted. Nick moved to protest, only
to be stood down. 'The Blue Hare is my home, let the Worthingtons
come should they wish. I'll be waiting. Besides, I might be able to
buy you some time,' she finished. Nick's concern was written across
his face, there was no arguing as she ushered him and his daughter
into the nearest car.

'Where are we heading to?' Luke asked.

'Back to London. We'll regroup there,' Gary ordered, his attention
caught by the flicker of some headlights framed between the nearby
hedgerows. 'We'll figure it out. Don't use your mobile phones.'

Aisha's hand trembled inside Luke's, he felt it squeezing tighter
with every second. In a moment of calm, he slid his spare hand
across to her right pocket and pulled out her phone. It was clumsy of
him, far too close he thought. Her eyes snapped to his instantly, then

drifted down. 'Sorry. It will be much safer this way,' Luke gruffed awkwardly. Aisha gripped even harder.

'Can we… can we go to Bushra's? In London?' she croaked.

'We'll do what we can,' Luke tried to reassure her. Adam shot a critical look over to his brother before tossing him the keys.

'Best you drive,' Adam asserted, while opening the passenger door.

'I'm not sure what would be worse. The White Dragon on our tails or having to sit here watching you attempt to drive us over to London,' Luke joked. Adam opened his mouth to respond just as the pop of a single bullet was heard, followed by a scream from Beth. The brothers looked on with alarm as Carl Bishop lay on his side a few metres away from his car, arm stretched out, dripping blood. Then motionless.

'Luke! *Drive!*' Adam shouted. Luke had already slammed in the gears as Violet tumbled into the back seat next to Aisha. 'Violet! Go with your dad,' Adam yelled over his shoulder.

'I… I can't get to him. He and Gary are pinned down,' Violet quivered. The sharp spark of bullets from Gary's car sprang up to their side as Luke floored the accelerator.

'There's only one road out of here,' Luke muttered, trying to find the front lights.

'We'll take our chances. Just draw them away from the others,' Adam replied, checking rear mirrors for any sign of Gary and Nick. The welcome sight of Graham's car pulled up behind them, Fernando ducking behind the dashboard as a volley of bullets struck their roof. Two grey vans flanked their exit to the main road ahead, Adam could see, and at least one more in pursuit.

'This is going to be tight.' Luke gritted his teeth. They accelerated through the rain of shots puncturing the chase. 'We're not going to make it, I can't see,' he winced as the windscreen shattered. Adam ventured a brief glimpse back to Graham and Fernando, under the same volley of fire. Their headlights swerved, Graham as the driver, possibly hit. Their car went crashing through the left hedgerow at top speed, bouncing wildly across the field.

'What's he doing?' Luke yelled.

'Just keep driving,' Adam instructed, trying to fix a location on Graham's car. Its trajectory became clear. He concentrated to summon his flaming spear, leaning his door open enough to get a clear shot. 'Heads down!'

Adam's conjured blue spear was hurled at the nearest oncoming van just as Graham collided with the second. Pillars of blue and orange fire pierced the sky, and the welcome smooth tarmac of the main road was under them. Luke breathed a deep sigh of relief. 'Everyone OK?' Violet and Aisha cautiously lifted their heads.

The twisted wreck of Graham's car was burning behind. Adam looked back, desperate to see if either McCreedy or Fernando were visible. Nothing. The grey van lay crumpled on its side, engulfed in smoke. Two beams of light broke through, the roar of an engine right behind them growing louder. Adam strained through the evening sky, hoping to see Gary and Nick. The urgency of the vehicle behind made him believe otherwise.

'Luke, get off this road,' Adam yelled.

'What? To where?' Luke panicked.

'Anywhere. Down that side road,' Adam pointed. Luke spun the wheel, jostling all inside. The van behind followed. More bullets came whistling past, striking the parked cars that flew by, glass whizzing in front of Luke.

'Jesus!' Luke winced. 'It's getting too narrow down here. Hang on.' He stamped hard on the brake, bringing the car to a sudden stop, the van behind reacting the same way, but with too little time. Its bumper clipped the rear end of theirs as it tried to turn, met with a signpost. All four jolted forward, Aisha giving a short scream with what little breath she had left.

'We're OK. Go, Luke, go!' Violet commanded, clinging to Aisha.

'It's not stopped them,' Adam confirmed as the van reversed, side light hanging down. It accelerated once more.

'Main road coming up again, Adam. Any more spears?' Luke nudged impatiently.

'I can't get the angle,' Adam replied. Several bullets started to find their mark, puncturing the dashboard and seats. Violet and Aisha hit the footwells once more. Adam managed to twist his torso around and bring his shield up in deflection, lighting up the interior in soft blue. 'I won't be able to hold this for long, Luke. What's up ahead?'

Luke peered ahead as the road began to widen. 'There's an overpass,' he replied.

'A what?'

'A road that goes over another road. Jeez,' Luke groaned. 'I have an idea. Can you shoot their tyres out?'

'What makes you think I can do that right now?' Adam snapped back, just about holding his balance.

'Fine. Take the wheel, will you.' Luke fumbled for his pistol in the holster. Adam levered himself into position.

'I can't do this with one hand, Luke. We'll lose the shield,' Adam warned.

'Just do it,' Luke insisted. He swung his door open, barely maintaining a foot on the accelerator, steadying himself with the slack of the safety belt. 'When I say so, turn to the right.'

'The overpass is coming up, Luke. I can't turn right,' Adam fired back. Luke remained quiet, his shoulder almost grazing the road below. 'Luke!'

Through clenched jaws, Luke shouted 'Now!' Adam didn't hesitate. The car veered to the right long enough for Luke to get off three clean shots, one finding the target. The van following them slumped as its front tyre blew out, a shower of sparks flew out from beneath it. The screech of brakes came, then the hot smell of rubber. The van slid to its side, then rolled over, buckling the railings of the overpass, coming to a stop.

Luke reeled himself in, rewarded with a hearty slap on the arm by Adam. Violet broke the collective sigh of relief. 'My dad. Is he still behind us?' Luke brought the car to a stop.

'I can't see them,' Adam noted. 'We need to keep moving.'

'But Adam. My dad, and Gary. They might need our...' Violet began.

'We can't stay, Violet. We've got to get out of here. Gary and

Nick will need to handle themselves.' Adam said. 'And we can't call them… not now.' Violet's eyes began to well up, and Aisha offered a gentle cuddle.

'Where in London are we supposed to go?' Aisha composed herself. 'Bushra's is the only place I would know.'

'We're not going there. Or to any of her friends or family.' Adam replied. 'Gary had a small place in Fleet Street, we can try there for now.'

'Sure the White Dragon won't know it?' Luke questioned. Adam shrugged. The car started up again. 'Not sure what's left of this piece of junk will get us to London.'

The back window suddenly shattered with a flurry of bullets from behind. The four threw themselves to the floor of the car, shouts and screams ringing. A lone survivor from the wrecked van, armed with a semi-automatic, limped his way towards them, his face oozing fresh blood over the crooked black headscarf, spitting out the words *'For Palamedes!'*

Adam rolled out, hand covering his head as he brought his shield of blue fire forward. His adrenaline pumped, absorbing round after round from the soldier, his strength ebbing away with each hit. The intensity was too much. He buckled to his knee, letting out a shout of defiance as the firepower focused on him. Relief came in an instant flash of pure pale light from behind, the ground beneath his feet immediately becoming unstable. He fell backwards as the road cracked open like an eggshell, the overpass rumbling then folding in two, billowing soot and bitter smoke as it collapsed onto the main road. Cars below began to skid to a halt, horns blaring then fading out. Adam coughed violently, clearing the dust from his throat, and called out. Through the clouds of smoke he saw a dim white light pulsing from Luke's hand, the gleam of Excalibur's blade barely distinguishable, its tip deep in the earth. His brother stood resting on its pommel, skin drained of colour. He turned just enough to make eye contact with Adam before falling helplessly to the floor. The sword returned to its recognisable wooden form once his hands slipped from it, falling into a pool of Luke's blood.

CHAPTER 14

---◆---

CARDIFF - ENGLAND
6th April 2012 AD

G ARY SLUMPED LOWER AGAINST HIS CAR AMIDST THE RATTLE OF gunfire. Every time he tried to peer around the side to gauge the distance between him and Nick and their attackers, dirt from bullets sprayed up in anticipation. His heart raced, muscles bunched up from adrenaline. He watched the second car speed away with Luke at the wheel, Adam, Violet and Aisha bundled inside. He strained to focus on its fading rear lights, they were coming under fire from what appeared to be two vans up ahead, but he couldn't be sure. They were on their own now.

Nick's solid hand landed on Gary's thigh. 'Violet's gone with them,' he shouted over the commotion, trying to mask his anxiety. 'How are we going to shake these bastards?' Gary raised his staff, the soft white light transforming it into a knight's sword. Beth was right, they could all buy the others some time.

'On my mark… blind them. Deflect what you can and try to get in close, close enough for a blade.' Gary grunted in agreement. Nick gave a weary smile and brought forth his own staff, sword newly revealed. They waited for a pause in the volley, a few snappy words in Arabic were heard together with the crunch of gravel under boots as the enemy advanced. Gary gave the order – 'Now!' – as he and Nick planted their blades into the ground for the brilliant knight light, the nearest of their foes shielding their eyes best they could. The swords cut through enemy flesh swiftly. One body, then two. The gunfire started up again from those told to hang back. Gary brought his sword down into the earth once more to summon momentary light, strong enough to repel a single salvo of fire, but not a second. The sharp pain of a shot into his left shin toppled him to the side and he frantically scrambled back into the safety of the car. 'Damn it. There are too many of them,' Gary cursed. Nick did not respond. He hauled himself to the front end of the car where he saw his fellow knight stand with him, craned his neck around to catch a glimpse of Nick's heavy frame lying on its side, sword still held high in a faint white glimmer, blood trickling down his arm.

'Nick. *Hold on*!' Gary shouted. He crawled over on his belly and anchored his forearm across Nick's barrel chest. Swords brought together to intensify their defence. He struggled to drag Butcher's body back to the car, his own wound now burning. His footing slipped, inches from the exposed tyres. Gary felt Nick's breath slow, the warmth of his blood now reaching the palm clamped below his breast. He couldn't make it back. They couldn't make it back. Gary collapsed by Nick's side, his sword's light dimming. He gazed at the evening sky, cherry-red, pierced with specks of early stars. The next wave of bullets would be the last, that much he knew. He dared close his eyes for a moment, and upon opening them again a single object shot across his vision. A small ball… a grenade perhaps? He didn't care now. Whether by bullet or bomb, the two knights' fate was sealed. But the trajectory of the ball was from behind them, not in front. Panic ensued among the gunmen, then a crisp orange explosion followed.

Gary rolled back onto his belly, bewildered. He could see Beth, frantically waving from behind the car. She was shouting, that much was clear, although he heard little because his ears were still ringing from the blast. She threw her arms out to meet Gary's, and the two reeled in Nick's body. 'You're OK, I've got you. Come on,' Beth said.

'What was that?' Gary coughed out. 'A grenade?'

'You honestly think during his visits over the years Nick didn't bring a few things over here?' Beth tutted. 'I only had the one, I'm afraid.' The two looked back to see all but a few armed soldiers dashing for the cover of their van amidst the scorching heat lingering from the blast. Those that were still standing tried to advance, but the explosions that roared from a distance were enough to send them away in pursuit. Beth turned towards the end of the pathway leading to the main road. 'They're going after the Allen boys,' she sighed.

'Violet? What... about... Violet?' Nick groaned, just managing to hold on to consciousness. Beth looked again and saw only a single car heading down the main road, no sign of the second. Was it Luke driving, or was it Graham McCreedy? Hard to tell, and even harder to share with Nick. She comforted Butcher with a gentle stroke of his beard. 'She'll be OK. We promise.' Gary continued to hold Nick close, his breath getting more shallow. Beth pressed her cardigan against the blood welling up on his belly, causing Nick to wince briefly.

'Was... was that my grenade?' Nick managed to choke out. Beth strained a chuckle through her tears and nodded. 'Told you... always go out with a bang,' he smiled back. He hooked his fingers over his wooden staff and pushed it towards Gary. 'This is my Violet's now. May she be the best Butcher of all.'

'Sir Bors the Butcher,' Gary croaked, weeping.

'There is no other kind.' Nick breathed heavily, then closed his eyes for the final time.

CHAPTER 15

⟫◈⟪

CARDIFF – WALES

6th – 21st April 2012 AD

ALL LUKE COULD FEEL WAS THE HEAT. EVERY INCH OF HIS BODY was on fire. No pain. He touched the soft fabric of the hospital bedding, soaked in sweat but providing an odd sense of comfort. Images came into his view as a haze, some logical, some incomprehensible. He recognised the kind face of Aisha, who was pressing a cool wet towel to his forehead, then his brother Adam towering over him speaking in what sounded like utter gibberish. A steady but inviting gaze from Violet, who was gripping his hand.

In between the flashes of white and blue nurses' uniforms came pictures far less familiar. At once he was transported back to a grand house shared with a slim gentleman, complete with dashing robes of silk, introducing him to another fine-looking man called Henry of Tudor. Luke failed to grasp the details of the conversation being exchanged, only something about a final battle on the fields of Bosworth that was due to take place soon. Henry offered him a bright crimson rose that instantly transformed itself into a small red dragon, squeaking playfully. Luke smiled, and responded by revealing the blade of Excalibur, quite at ease it would seem, though how he was unsure. It delighted Henry and his company, but they provided a harsh warning of the white rose counterparts under the banner of Richard of York, why they must be stopped for the good of England. The small red dragon crouched in the corner of Luke's vision as its fierce white counterpart came into sight.

The prick from a hypodermic needle dispersed the scene. Encouragement from Aisha and Violet to stay focused and listen to their voices led to another encounter. A grizzly-looking face surrounded by eighteenth-century militia appeared around a hardy oak table. Luke recognised this one. Ulysses S. Grant, doffing his cap to the Union Flag perched high above. His hands, however, were not his own, at least as far as he could recognise. He was African, or African-American, the handle of Excalibur just about covering the scars of shackles on his wrists. Perhaps a relative of Mack Benson, he thought, as he caught sight of his reflection in an ornate mirror.

Adam's voice was now heard, and his brother appeared in front of him once more. Concern was etched across his face, Violet visible in the background next to Gary. She was crying uncontrollably into Gary's chest, with Beth trying to console her. Luke felt anger for the first time, he was helpless, but wanted nothing more than to rush over and be by Violet's side. He arched his back in frustration, and Aisha promptly soothed him. She got him to close his eyes, breathe deeply, then open them slowly. He did as he was told, and saw nothing but torn fields of mud. He was in a trench, the stench of decay engulfing him, curdling his stomach.

There was panic all around. Men wearing First World War uniforms darted past him with fear in their faces. One shouted his name – Ben Benson, an officer – and asked for orders. Luke had none, only the instinct to run. He gripped his pistol and was tempted to point it to the underside of his chin, if it weren't for the display of gallantry on display before him. The familiar blue circle of flame from what he knew to be a Sacred Band warrior, successfully drawing fire from the German guns. He had to run, otherwise this warrior's brave actions would have been for nothing. Luke ran as fast as he could, following the shouts from his comrades into the dense canopy of nearby trees. 'Hell's last issue, reduced to fleeing,' he anguished. Now the pain came.

Luke stopped to catch his breath, leaning against the bruised bark of a fallen tree. The tree transformed itself into human form, causing him to stumble back in horror. The cold, hardened complexion of Lady Morgan greeted him, silver hair flowing, her ashen gown barely covering her breasts. 'Such a burden is the king's blade, my dear Master Allen, son of Galahad,' she whispered over the wind. 'Please, let me take it for you. Spare the pain the sons of Bedivere endured, what your friend Mack Benson and his family endured. There is no need for it now.' Her icy fingers stretched out towards Excalibur, suddenly in Luke's hands once more. His mind was at war with itself, the temptation to relinquish the sword to Morgan le Fay and be done with all the suffering he'd experienced overwhelming. He thought of Mary Cassidy, their friend Jennifer Van Hansen, his mother Elaine, his father Richard. What if they could all be spared by this one act of capitulation – surely it was worth it. His arms began to rise and meet with Morgan le Fay's, Excalibur pulsing vibrantly against the red jewel radiating out just below the sorceress's throat. He cast his gaze down, and in Morgan le Fay's other hand was the Palladium, the small feminine statue carved in honour of the beloved friend of Athena, the Greek goddess of wisdom. The source of all Mary's pain. His family's pain. *His* pain. Luke let out a tremendous roar of defiance, and swung Excalibur with all his might at Lady Morgan, her expression showing both awe and anger at the sight of the blade's full force. She disappeared behind a veil of thin, green smoke as its edge reached her neck. Luke was alone.

'Very dramatic,' said a calm voice from behind. Luke spun round. Mary was standing just as she did when he had last seen her in the flesh, the seas of the Cornish coast stretching out behind her, the scent of brine washing up from beneath coupled with a warm ocean breeze.

'You're not about to fall again, are you Min?' Luke asked, surprising himself with his assurance. 'Not sure I could watch it a second time.'

'Not this time, babe,' Mary smiled. 'Certainly put you and your brother through it though, haven't I?'

'You could say that.'

'Well, it was never my intention. Nor was it Adam's, or Richard's or your mother's,' Mary replied.

'What makes you think I was trying to shift the blame?' Luke asked.

'Because that's what you always do, Luke. Trust me, it does no one any favours… least of all those who wield the king's blade,' Mary said. Luke looked down at Excalibur thoughtfully.

'Why did you give this to me, Min? I'm no Knight of the Round Table, despite my parents. You know me, better than *anyone*.' Luke pressed.

'Indeed I do. Do you think I made a mistake?'

'Never known you to. You were the smartest person I knew. That anyone knew,' Luke gushed. Mary managed a coy blush.

'Then why don't you trust me?' she asked.

'Because this is… this is nonsense, Min. I just want us to be together again, as we were in Boston. With Jenny and my mother. It wasn't a perfect life, but it was our life,' Luke defended. 'I've never been involved in the crazy world of magic and knights, of witches and wizards, maddening tales of Ancient Greece and King Arthur. That was my father's world, and Adam's. Not ours.'

Mary took a few tentative steps forward. 'Luke Allen. You cannot be that naïve. After everything you've witnessed, what makes you think we were ever going to be safe from this power? Has anyone over the millennia not been impacted in some way by the Trinity?' she posed.

Luke focused on her last words. The *Trinity*. Morgan le Fay had spoken similar words in the tomb of King Arthur, during their encounter in Edinburgh. Pieces of the puzzle began to lock into place.

'The Palladium you found, aboard the Bismarck, that's one part of the Trinity?' Luke proposed.

'The power to forge empires – *birth* if you will,' Mary confirmed.

'That necklace Lady Morgan wears… that's another.'

'The Necklace of Harmonia, born of greed and desire, typical of *life,* wouldn't you say? Never far from the Palladium, always drawn to it… like Morgan le Fay is now. Just like desire itself, it can keep its wearer quite, well, *motivated* shall we say.' Mary smirked.

'As in immortal?' Luke suggested.

'Not quite, as I'm sure you've worked out. But certainly youthful. You are talking about a sorceress that is as old as time. Just like leaves on an autumn tree back home in Boston, they will always wither and fade eventually.' Luke recalled the moment when Violet tore the jewel away from Lady Morgan, and her resulting distress.

'And this?' Luke raised the gleaming blade of Excalibur. 'The third piece of the puzzle?' he gave a wry smile.

'The bringer of *death.* Of course.'

'*Death*?' Luke blurted.

'It's not necessarily a bad thing, Luke. Think of it as *letting go.* Something everyone has to come to terms with should they wish for a stable mind. Poor Mack Benson and his family had a tough time of it, most of the Sir Bedivere bloodline has over the centuries, my predecessor Jane DuLac informed me. A constant battle over guilt from wrongs done, having to understand the difficult lesson of *learning* from mistakes, not punishing yourself for them,' Mary continued. 'In the right hands… the bringer of death can actually end suffering as a natural part of life. Allow new growth, as from winter comes spring.'

'In the right hands, Min. How do you know that's me?' Luke tried once more.

'Seriously? You think it to be Morgan le Fay's? A soul so deprived of love for anyone or anything other than herself, could she understand the *true* meaning of sacrifice? Those that come to successfully wield the might of Excalibur must first *know* what it is to love, and be prepared to die for that love. The love of something, or someone more than yourself. Simply *witnessing* it is not enough. Morgan le Fay considers love to be a weakness in mankind, when it is anything but. It was the destiny of those sons and daughters of Sir Bedivere to try and come to know this since the days of King Arthur… and in doing so, would bring to an end some of the worst atrocities known to this world. Atrocities born of the Palladium and the Necklace of Harmonia,' Mary replied.

Luke thought of William Wood, of his love Karen Milligan, the knights Sir Gawain and Sir Kay. William first witnessing Karen's death from the roof of the Imperial War Museum, her final words of sacrifice. He too must have understood by the time it came to shielding Violet from Colonel Thorpe's bullet, the act of loving your family and friends more than your own life, enough to give Mack Benson the strength to swing the very blade Luke himself has struggled with until now. Did he know such sacrifice? Wait… of course he did, he was looking right at it. At this very spot here in Tintagel. Where his love Mary Cassidy would rather fall to her death than be the vessel that brought the Palladium directly into Morgan le Fay's hands once more. 'Penny now dropping for you, hun?' Mary cracked a grin. Luke responded with a relieved one of his own.

'Wait. It's over then, isn't it? Lady Morgan can't win, not if she can't wield Excalibur, as you say? She doesn't love or care. Why can't we just continue as before?' Luke pleaded.

'Just as the Red and White Dragon factions have done for over ten thousand years. You know the definition of madness, don't you, babe?' Mary shook her head. 'No. This all must stop. Lady Morgan and her artefacts of destruction must be destroyed.'

'But what can she do? You just said she'll never wield all three.'

'She can change the board. Channel strength from a time even the great wizard Merlin feared. A time of ancient power, free of the ingrained beliefs of many of today's cherished religions. At the dawn of the transit of Venus, when the female element is at its strongest, the Trinity could still be used to devastating effect. If she cannot sit on the throne, bend the minds of man and ensure their following, then you can be sure retribution will be swift, uncontrollable perhaps.' Mary flared. 'Then…'

'Checkmate.' Luke said without hesitation. Violet had taught him that much through their sessions of chess. 'Can we stop her?'

'Not without risk. The transit will bring Morgan le Fay power, but also a newfound weakness as she opens up to her own source of power in the presence of the Trinity – her *own* creation, life and death laid all before her, in a sense being reborn. We're always at our most vulnerable when born for the first time – *nature's way*,' Mary said.

The enormity of the task in hand struck Luke. To emerge victorious, he would have to do the unthinkable, offer Excalibur to Morgan le Fay. But then, he knew no more. He drew in a breath as he heard Adam's voice echoing in the distance, he turned in every direction but couldn't see him. 'Min, what about you? Will you be, you know, ok?' Luke asked tenderly.

'You know me, hun, I'm always at home when in the water.' Mary's smile warmed Luke as a cold spray from the sea splashed up and met his face. She was gone.

CHAPTER 16

———◆◇◆———

CARDIFF – WALES

21st April, 2012 AD

'YOU DON'T HALF TALK A LOT IN YOUR SLEEP.' AISHA SMILED AS she soothed Luke's forehead with a cool towel. He forced a smile back, but was lost in thought, blinking in time with the slow bleep of the heart monitor casting a soft glow beside them.

'What time is it?' Luke inquired.

'Just after nine o'clock.' Aisha consulted her watch.

'Morning or evening?'

'Evening,' she chuckled while drawing the curtain back to reveal a dark sky framed by the window. 'You've been here for about two weeks. The wound in your side is healing nicely, so the doctors tell us.'

Luke shifted to try and get comfortable on the bed, pressing his fingers against the gauze that covered his right side. He bit his lip in sharp pain. 'You tell them what happened?' he asked nervously.

'Adam thought on his feet. The entire incident he described as an accident... one minute we were all in the car, the next, the whole overpass collapsed. Will probably be an inquiry over the safety of roads all over Wales now,' Aisha grinned. Luke scanned the room for his brother. It was only the two of them. Luke opened his mouth to ask about Adam and Violet's whereabouts when he saw a small picture in Aisha's hand. He recognised it instantly – his photograph of Mary and Jenny, the crude scribbles of Jenny's old phone number faded but still visible. 'You were holding this a lot when you were talking. Mentioned Mary Cassidy and Jenny Van Hansen... I know you spoke about them briefly earlier and, well, just guessed this might have been them?' Aisha offered the passport strip to Luke.

Their grins echoed another world now, Mary in her polka dots and Minnie Mouse ears, him with the poorly fitting Santa beard. It had all appeared so carefree. Luke clutched the pictures in his hand and uttered an uneasy thank you. Aisha comforted him with her fingers lightly running across his arm, before catching the IV drip needle, causing him to flinch briefly. Before she could utter an apology Luke disarmed her with a playful snigger.

'Welcome back to the land of the living,' Adam appeared from behind the curtain, half-empty water bottle stuffed in his pocket. 'Was a bit touch-and-go there, brother. Sorry, am I interrupting?' he caught a glimpse of Aisha's hand atop of Luke's.

'No...*no*. Not at all. I'll go check on Violet and Gary.' Aisha cleared her throat while composing herself. Adam took her seat and pulled out from behind him the smooth wooden staff he'd concealed under his jacket.

'Probably still best in your hands.' Adam passed the staff over to Luke. 'Managed to keep it safe. You'll be pleased to hear I had no luck wielding it,' he said.

'Well, that makes two of us then, doesn't it.' Luke frowned.

'Not really. Do you remember what happened on the overpass?' Adam enquired. Luke shook his head hesitantly.

'I remember a lot of pain. A lot of anger. Then...' Luke began.

'Then, what?'

'Min. Min appeared. Just like she did in Scotland. I... I couldn't explain it. Any of it, Adam.' Luke stuttered.

'Try.' Adam insisted.

'She was just... *there*. Just as we'd last seen her at Tintagel. But, calm. She explained something about a Trinity, three sacred objects, this – Excalibur – being one.' Luke continued.

Adam put his chin in his hands. 'The others being the Palladium and the Necklace of Harmonia? Jesus… Mum and Dad were right,' he sighed. Luke looked at him, puzzled. 'You don't remember the little riddle they shared with us when we were growing up? During the whole 'Excalibur being pulled from the stone of destiny' game. The Ballad of the Trinity, I think Dad called it. The one that started *Those that know love, but feel its true pain…?'*

'Sort of.' Luke gave a casual shrug while racking his morphine-addled memory for a trace of anything like it.

'It was all part of a legend dating back to the founding of Thebes by Cadmus. When Athena first entrusted him and his warriors with the task of guarding that which was most precious to her, the Palladium, carved in honour of her dear friend Pallas,' Adam explained. Luke dropped his head back into his pillow, preparing himself for another mythical lecture. Adam did his best to offer him the abridged version of events – the curse Ares placed upon his betrothed daughter Harmonia, the well where the Sacred Band was born, and the waters they drank to imbue them with strength for generations. Undone by Alexander the Great, with his insatiable thirst for land and power driven by Harmonia's necklace, forever entwined with the Palladium. Empire after empire, rising and falling.

'And somewhere along the line, Morgan le Fay got her hands on both of them,' Luke interjected with impatience.

'We know it as possibly the First Crusade, Dad would say,' Adam replied. 'The quest undertaken by Sir Percival, Sir Gawain and Sir Galahad – the quest for the *Grail.*'

'Uh-huh.' Luke scoffed at the notion. He then heard Mary's words in his head from the dream – the Trinity of birth, life and death. A foundation of all faiths in some form. A chill went down his bed-sored spine… suddenly this didn't appear that far-fetched.

'The Palladium and the Necklace together in Arthurian Britain, with Morgan le Fay in complete command, twisting the minds of King Arthur and his son Mordred into fatal conflict. Splitting the

Round Table into the Red and White, differing divisions of loyalty. At war through the ages. The only defence against such power being…' Adam gestured towards the wooden staff in Luke's hands.

'Death,' Luke said coldly, in a trance. Adam was taken aback at his choice of word for Excalibur. 'So… what now?'

'I was hoping you'd be able to tell us.' Adam puffed out his chest. 'You, after all, have been the only one to come close to wielding the king's blade.'

'You're not going to like my answer.' Luke closed his eyes in resignation. Adam waited. 'We need to give it to her. Excalibur. Hand it over to Lady Morgan.'

Adam's face dropped. 'I'll come back later, when the sedatives have worn off,' he said crassly.

'I'm serious bro. Let her have it. Only that way can we stop her,' Luke insisted. Adam stood up and turned to leave. 'Otherwise, we're just destined to repeat everything Mum and Dad did, and our whole bloodline of Sir Galahad. Lady Morgan rises with the Palladium and the Necklace of Harmonia, the bloodline of Sir Bedivere sometimes rises to the challenge with Excalibur – again and again. From Henry Tudor to the American Civil War, it just goes on and on. When are you and your cannon-fodder boyfriends going to get it? Things must *change*,' Luke spat with delirious agitation. It was enough to bring Adam to a halt.

'Did you just call the Sacred Band *cannon-fodder*?' Adam creased his brow in disapproval. His brother flicked his hand dismissively.

'You're just too loyal, bro. To Dad, the Red Dragon, to that traitor Iain Donnelly. You don't question whether things are right or wrong… it's only what's played out in front of you. Make up your own mind for once!' Luke bristled. Adam clenched his fist as the image of Iain flashed into his mind. His partner had held Excalibur once too, pain etched across his face as he limped away from King Arthur's tomb, unable to wield it against him. Of all the men capable of lifting such a weapon, Adam wanted it to be Iain. Call it an overly romantic notion, whatever Adam knew of such things. Watching him struggle as its handle weighed on him, felt as if his heart was being twisted.

Both Mack Benson, and now his own brother Luke, harboured a deep-rooted feeling Iain didn't or perhaps wasn't prepared to accept. Blinded by his ambition to correct the world and all the wrongs it had done him, Iain had never appreciated the very love Adam gave him. He would possibly never have understood what it would have meant if Adam was to have willingly fallen at the hands of a blue-flamed spear. *Possibly.*

The darkness of his thoughts enveloped Adam. He briefly rubbed the scar on his collarbone, raw as the day Iain inflicted it, jutted out his jaw but held his composure, as he so often had done despite the internal conflict, and walked away. He brushed past Gary and Violet. 'You talk to him!'

Luke noted Violet's eyes, moist with tears, and let his intuition flow as to the whereabouts of her father. A firm embrace was the only gift he could offer.

CHAPTER 17

BATH – ENGLAND

27th January 2012 AD

'W HEN WAS THAT?' IAIN ASKED SOFTLY. 'THE BATTLE OF Chaeronea?'

'338 BC. Not sure of the specific date,' Adam replied, cheek resting against Iain's bare chest, tapping his fingers just above his nipple in rhythm to his heartbeat.

'Ah. And they all died? To the last man?' Iain continued.

'The Sacred Band did, yes. Some say they may even have killed each other, their partners, rather than capitulate to Philip II and his son Alexander.' Adam replied.

'Alexander *the Great.*' Iain smirked. 'Got to wonder how great the lad would have been had it not been for the Palladium, don't you?'

'He was still a very skilled general, Iain. Capable of wiping out Thebes, remember. And if you believe some accounts, Alexander himself noted a thing or two of what it was to be a Sacred Band warrior. Let's not forget his own best general, Hephaestion,' Adam spoke through a yawn. Their sparring session only moments earlier had drained them both, but for the briefest of moments, their strength was at its peak, they both felt it. Vivid blue fire forming both shield and spear, this was the first time Adam had summoned such a weapon, drawn out from ebullient rage and passion. The moment his father Richard and Karen Milligan had left the two of them, the rage subsided, the passion did not.

Iain winced as Adam's hand brushed a bruise on his hip. 'Sorry.' Adam smiled. 'That was a hell of a fall you took.'

'Tell me about it, lad.' Iain shifted position. 'Can't believe Richard made us use actual swords. I mean, *sharpened* swords.'

'That would have been the Spartan way. The *agoge* was done at a much younger age than us. Barely teenagers.' Adam laid his head back on Iain's chest. He noticed a small scar just below his rib cage and poked it gingerly. 'Where did you get this?'

'Ah, long time ago, lad. Was only young.' Iain sighed, closing his eyes for a moment in rest.

'How?'

'Well, let's just say my dad wasn't so accepting of all this stuff as yours is,' Iain said pensively.

'You're kidding. Your father did this?'

'As I said, long time ago, lad.' Iain tried to switch subjects. Adam wasn't letting go, not now. He wanted to know everything about Iain, past and present.

'Do you still see him? Your parents?' Adam inquired.

'Nah, left 'em ages ago back in Dublin. They might still be there, might not,' came Iain's dismissive response.

'Never tried to contact them?'

'No point. Unless I was going to leave a message with God's receptionist. Probably the only way they'd listen.' Iain stretched with a chuckle.

'You miss them?' Adam pressed.

'Not really. Well…sort of, but what can you do, eh? Kicked me out of home, so not exactly expecting a reunion anytime soon, lad.'

'Where did you go?'

'Just made my own way I guess. From place to place like. Working odd jobs and that. Got friendly with a few unsavoury characters, but they paid well.' Iain scratched his ginger stubble, trying to recall details.

Adam sat up, rolled his sore shoulder a few times before asking, 'The Worthingtons? Sir Lawrence and Lady Morgan. How did you come to know them?'

'Jeez, sounding like an interview now, lad.' Iain laughed, bringing his hand to Adam's jaw. 'If you must know, a friend offered me a job catering these fancy dinner parties and events. Always a good way of meeting people of influence, thought it sounded like a good idea. Never know when these people might need a bodyguard or something.'

Adam put his hand on Iain's. 'You knew you were Sacred Band then? Thought you'd put your skills to good use?' Adam pressed.

'Something like that, yeah. Wasn't sure about all this Greek warrior business, but knew I was strong, healed up pretty quick from bar fights and such. I think that Lady Morgan saw something in me pretty early on, like.' Iain kept eye contact. Such a candid yet open-ended explanation of his connection to Sir Lawrence and Lady Morgan fuelled Adam's desire to probe further.

'Did you know about the two of them? Their ancestry? Sir Lawrence, born of the Knights of Lancelot and Lady Morgan, well…' Adam looked crestfallen.

'Some sorceress? Ha! She's an odd one, I'll give you that much, lad, but thought her more of a Houdini than a Gandalf. Great with kids, strange she and Sir Lawrence never had any of their own, I thought.' Iain smiled. Now there was a thought, Adam considered – whether Lady Morgan had ever had children of her own, or indeed Sir Lawrence had every desired any. The line of Sir Lancelot would have had to live on somehow after all these generations. Maybe his wife dictated that very aspect of Sir Lawrence's life also, encouraging infidelity for her personal gain. She, after all, would live on if the tales were to be believed. Such a thought was almost enough to make Adam feel sorry for Sir Lawrence Worthington -- a mere puppet king for the White Dragon.

'I don't believe Lady Morgan capable of caring enough for children of her own,' Adam broke in.

'You think?' Iain doubted.

'Absolutely. I won't confess to knowing all that my father has seen over his years heading up the Red Dragon and fighting against Lady Morgan, but he has never once described her as anything other than selfish. I mean, look what she's inflicted on the world over the centuries,' Adam retorted.

Iain cast a quizzical look in Adam's direction. 'Is the line of Sir Galahad so noble? What of the others in the Red Dragon? Never shed any blood of others for personal gain? Ever wondered whether both sides are equally guilty?' Iain posed. Adam recalled a similar approach from his partner upon travelling down to Tintagel, he didn't want to believe it then and didn't want to believe it now... the notion that his father and his loyal friends might also be part of the problem, the endless cycle of destruction witnessed for so many years. He drove the thought out of his mind, as before.

'I know where I should stand,' Adam's stoic response came again.

Iain sat up and brought his lips to Adam's forehead. 'Remember lad, you're Sacred Band, not Sir Galahad or Knight of the Round Table. You might need to think wider, not accept things just as they are. People in this world suffer in more ways than you can know, not just at the hands of some old Greek statue and a pretty necklace,' he whispered. Adam lowered his chin to rest on Iain's shoulder, picking up the scent of fresh sweat from his back. He nuzzled the shaven stubble on the nape of his neck and thought, no more debate tonight. But one gnawing question remained, one Adam needed Iain to answer.

'All this fighting, these wars. Would you give it all up for me? If you had to?' Adam asked bluntly. Iain pulled Adam's head away and pressed his hands either side of his face with that same cocky grin that made Adam blush each time.

'Of course, lad. Of course.'

CHAPTER 18

─────◈─────

CARDIFF - WALES

1st June 2012 AD

AVING SPENT THE BEST PART OF THREE WEEKS ENTANGLED IN debate and grievances from what was now the closest to what she could call a family, Violet Butcher was pleased to escape the turmoil for a few hours and sit peacefully on vales overlooking the River Severn. The hazy evening sun played with the mackerel skies, a few swallows swooped into view as she lay on her back and nestled into the damp grass.

The scent of summer blooms always reminded her of her mother and the trails the two used to blaze in the local forests this time of year when she was a child. She could name every type of mushroom by the age of six, even if their pronunciation was sometimes a struggle, then by her tenth birthday, she was on to birds and butterflies. Her mother comforted her during her final days, when walking in the woods became laboured, telling her that even though birds migrate for months at a time, they always find their way home. Out of sight was never out of mind. She had done a lot of growing up since then with her father, taking over the chores her mother once did with a precocious charm. She continued to study, was near the top in her classes, and upon turning fifteen could pull a pint of Guinness better than anybody, according to William Wood and Karen Milligan. Now that was an achievement.

William Wood, Karen Milligan, now her own father Nick Butcher – all gone. She dug her nails into the soil to try and purge the thought, tortured further upon realising that no one had really had a chance to say a formal goodbye to any of them yet. No funerals, no gatherings, no mourning. All too risky, Gary Willis said. She understood, but that didn't make things any easier.

Could she run a pub on her own? The Bear would need a new owner. She felt as if she owed it to all of them, and to Richard Allen, to keep the pub alive. Perhaps with Beth's help? Maybe put her own stamp on the tired building, given the furniture was looking worn now, several comfy seats stained and the fabric splitting. No one wanted to sit on those, she thought, especially now with, well, *bullet holes* in them.

'You keep leaving this on Gary's kitchen table,' came Aisha's mellow voice. Her father's wooden staff came into view. Violet couldn't help but screw her eyes shut. 'It's yours now, your dad wanted you to have it,' Aisha reminded her.

'What if I don't want it?' Violet spurned, turning away. Aisha took a seat by her side and lightly tugged on the stray strands of Violet's beige crop. 'Stop it, that tickles!' she snipped.

'Just good to see you can still smile,' Aisha laughed. 'Not seen much of it these past few days.

'I'm just fed up with all the arguing. Luke, Adam, Gary – that bloody Excalibur sword!' Violet grumbled. 'Part of me just wishes they would give the thing to Lady Morgan and Sir Lawrence Worthington and just be done with it. Let's go back to our own lives. I'm sick of it.'

Aisha placed her father's wooden staff on Violet's lap. 'Do you think that's what your dad would have wanted?' she asked.

'Really don't care. I'm not my father.'

'I would imagine a lot of those born into this particular world say that. Not sure we can change who we are.' Aisha replied. 'Trust me, I certainly don't want to become *my father.*'

Violet curled her fingers round her father's staff, pretended to thrust it into a foe with force, only to feel clumsy. It would have been easy to bear ill will to Aisha and her parents. The daughter of Mohammed Hussin and the line of Sir Palamedes, hands stained with more blood than maybe even the Worthingtons, and the cause of such pain to those closest to her. Aisha was not the enemy though, nor was her mother, just victims of circumstances. In Aisha however, she could see a newfound sense of purpose, a duty that Violet too had to master to correct the errors made by poor choices in her bloodline. The descendants of the Round Table couldn't make amends for all the wrongs their predecessors might have perpetrated, but each person born could make their own choices.

'Have you heard anything from your friend? Bushra?' Violet enquired.

'She's OK. Back with her family. Still shaken up of course but otherwise doing well,' Aisha said, now admiring the same view. 'Consider that a positive. I have no idea what my father might have done.'

'You think it was him?'

'Maybe not in person, but no doubt by his hand. I think the whole incident at The Blue Hare and with the Allen brothers just proved that one.' She gave an uncomfortable smile.

'Certainly dedicated followers he's got there,' Violet huffed.

'Always was wedded to his work, never us. Now I see why.' Aisha sighed.

'He's going to be there, isn't he? Your dad. If we travel to Mount Sinai, as Luke and Adam want us to,' Violet posed. Aisha pondered for a moment before playfully replying.

'If he is, he and I shall be having stern words!' she chuckled. 'Come on, let's get back to Gary's. See what the latest is on our travel plans, heaven help us.' Aisha hauled Violet to her feet.

Dragging her father's staff behind her, it dawned on Violet just how cumbersome the item was. How would she wield a knight's blade like he did? It felt too awkward and completely harmless, unlike a shotgun – now that felt more her style, that time in The Bear, apart from the fact the kickback almost floored her.

'You think if we go to Mount Sinai and encounter your father, along with Lady Morgan and Sir Lawrence, we'll get to have guns?' Violet proposed eagerly. 'Adam always said the world has changed… no point in all this sword and sandal stuff anymore.'

'Adam's powers are a little different, Violet.' Aisha reminded.

'True. But Luke… he's got the right idea, surely.' Violet replied, pointing the staff like a rifle and making shooting sounds. Aisha rolled her eyes, and in doing so left herself emotionally exposed. 'Luke, do you… y'know, quite like him?' Violet teased.

Aisha cracked a coy grin. 'I don't think he's ready for anything like that right now. Not after Mary.' she dismissed.

'But you do like him?' Violet pushed.

'Would that be a problem?'

Violet stopped to consider the question. Sure, Luke and she had grown close recently, how could they not? Adam of course was always like a big brother to her, and now with Luke being a part of the family once more, it was more like gaining another brother than having a crush on someone, she thought. More a second opinion, an extra voice to bring logic to her often scatty mental processes. Never romantic… nah, just didn't feel right.

She shook her head in response.

'We have three days.' Gary gestured with his fingers inches away from Luke's face. 'Three days before the transit of Venus, and we're still arguing about this.'

Luke heard the door from downstairs, immediately placing his hand on Excalibur. It had become a reflex. He relaxed as Aisha and Violet entered the kitchen. 'Where have you two been?' he enquired in an accusatory tone.

'Just out. Can you blame us?' Aisha soothed, helping herself to a digestive biscuit out of the packet on the kitchen table. 'Still tearing the flesh off one another, I see.'

Gary folded his arms, chin buried into his chest. 'I can't support this, Luke, you know I can't. Handing Excalibur over to Lady Morgan is reckless. We don't know what it might do.' He let out an exasperated sigh. 'Everything we've fought to protect, what your father died for, could be lost.'

'You don't think I know that, Gary? It's a risk, but what's the alternative? We stay here and wait for the White Dragon to come after us all again? More of us die along the way? Maybe we fight them off once more, maybe twice more – who knows? But sooner or later we've got to stop running. Make a *stand*.' Luke brought his palms together in a plea.

'Just last year, Luke, you had nothing to do with any of this, you led your own life in America. Now you think you know how all this works?' Gary fired back. 'You're incapable of making such decisions!'

Luke waved the smooth wooden bough of Excalibur in reply. 'I don't see you holding this!' His cocky demeanour triggered an eruption from Willis and a slew of comments and gesturing that took even Adam by surprise. He brought a small circle of blue fire to his wrist and wedged himself between the bigger Gary and his brother.

'Enough! Both of you, please.' Adam commanded.

'Bro, you know I'm right. I told you about Min. What she said in my dreams while I was in hospital,' Luke begged. Adam tried to remain impartial but knew there was some twisted logic to Luke's offer. He wanted clarity though, he always did. *Minimise the risk* his father always told him, wherever he was sent. Do your homework too – might just save your life. On this occasion, however, there was no textbook he could read or website he could search for. They would be taking a chance, and the odds were fifty-fifty. Not his preferred position.

'Tell me again, why do you think Lady Morgan can't wield Excalibur?' Adam quietly asked, the very question causing a lump to form in his throat. He knew the answer, at least he felt he did.

Luke's laconic and passive response, 'I just do,' brought a frown to Gary's face.

'Adam, no one has brought all three elements of the Trinity together before, as far as we know. Richard always feared it, hell, it was a fear born as far back as the Round Table itself. King Arthur trusted the Knights of Sir Bedivere to find and summon the king's blade when it was needed most, but *always to return* it to the Lady of the Lake until its time came again. Our ancestors knew its power, its danger. It's exactly what Lady Morgan wants us to do – give Excalibur up and hand her all the cards.' Gary tossed Carl Bishop's research down on the table, papers and photographs fluttering to the floor. 'We going to let them all down after hundreds of years?'

'You *have* been letting them down over hundreds of years!' Luke acerbically challenged, close to incurring a sharp fist to the jaw from Gary. Adam pulled the two apart again and tried to be rational once more.

'Lady Morgan didn't seem in control when she was holding Excalibur in Arthur's tomb. It clearly took a toll on her. Now maybe, maybe it exposes some form of weakness in her, especially if without the Necklace of Harmonia,' Adam suggested.

'I don't think she's going to fall for that again, Adam.' Gary sat back down, tapping his staff against the table leg. 'No offence, Violet.'

'None taken,' Violet chirped, brushing some biscuit crumbs off her sweater.

'Maybe we don't have to concern ourselves with this Trinity itself – the Palladium, the Necklace of Harmonia and Excalibur. We know the transit of Venus has been chosen for a reason by Lady Morgan. If she wants to bring about her New World Order, or the Old Ways as she calls it, it must require a great of her strength to do so, wouldn't you say?' Luke interjected.

'You're still clutching at a very, *very* few straws, Luke.' Gary stood firm. 'All of history would appear to disagree with you.'

'You just said no one's done it before, including Lady Morgan. So how do we know?' Luke sparked.

Adam now spoke, leaning into the back of his chair. 'The one thing we can be sure of is that we are going to be hopelessly outmatched by the White Dragon and all Sir Lawrence's and Mr Hussin's forces. We have one knight, a knight in training, one Sacred Band member and the *man-who-would-be-king* but can't work out how to use his sword to take on what could be a whole army.' He flustered, working his way around the group.

'I'm getting better,' Luke defended himself.

'You brought down a bridge and almost died, Luke!' Adam shot back. Aisha couldn't help but grin a little at Luke's wounded expression and his casual correction of his younger brother, that the proper term was "overpass". The doorbell rang downstairs.

'I'll get it,' Aisha insisted, seizing on this excuse to escape the seemingly interminable discussion. Luke put his hand on Adam's shoulder in mute accord.

'Adam, I know you doubt me. I understand why. I was a jerk back at the hospital… to you, and about Iain. Please trust me bro, I know this is right. Mary spoke to me, we can *win* if we do this,' he whispered softly.

'It's a big gamble, Luke. Too big. Gary is right, we can't take the risk,' Adam conceded.

'Would Dad have taken it?' Luke wondered.

'Almost certainly not…' Adam began to assert, before realising he'd walked into his brother's trap. 'I see what you're doing, Luke.'

'Still taking orders as always. Even when Dad's passed on,' Luke smiled. Adam shot a sharp look in his brother's direction, then admitted defeat.

'Gary, I'm with Luke. We need to try. I'd rather say to my father we at least tried to change history, not just repeat it.' Adam turned to Willis just as Aisha threw the door open.

'Guys… you might want to get down here,' she quivered.

Fernando was looking dishevelled, his curly black locks out of sorts, sticking out in all directions now they were not glued down by hair products. He looked tired, but with a strange determination written across his face. 'Sirs, m'ladies. I hope I am not disturbing. It took a long time to track your home down, Mr Willis, sir.' He tried his best English in spite of Violet squeezing the air from his lungs in a tight hug.

'Where have you been, Fernando? We lost you during the fight at The Blue Hare. Assumed you'd either fled or worse, been killed.' Gary gave a hearty sigh of relief.

'I know, so sorry, sir. It's just after Mr McCreedy, Graham, sir, after he died... I didn't know what to do.' Fernando stammered through choked-back tears. Aisha wrapped a welcome arm across his shoulder. 'He told me to run, and I didn't want to but... I had to obey him, sir. I wanted to help him but he was...'

'It's OK, Fernando, you're safe now.' Adam took his hand. 'You fought well.'

'Thank you, Mr Allen, sir. And Mr Willis, I did not use my phone, as you suggested,' Fernando confirmed. Gary nodded his approval.

'May I ask where you have been these past few weeks?' Luke inquired. Fernando produced Graham's scruffy notebook that listed so many Sacred Band members over the years.

'Recruiting, sir. Just as Graham had been doing, and asked me to continue just before he...' Fernando couldn't bring himself to say it.

Luke took the book from his hand and flicked through the pages, trying to decipher the scribbles. 'How many?'

'Not all, sir. Some no longer in contact, but others... including a brother of Mr William Wood,' Fernando replied. Luke and Adam looked at one another quizzically before turning to Gary.

'William had a brother?' Luke asked.

'Chris. Chris Wood, slightly older and never rallied to the cause despite several failed attempts by William. Assumed he'd given up after all these years... became something in the City of London I believe?' Gary shared.

'A stockbroker, sir. Yes,' Fernando confirmed.

'Bill rarely spoke of him to us, considered it a failure on his part that he never won him over. Too much valour, that man.' Gary shook his head.

Adam scratched the stubble on his neck. The bloodlines of both

Galahad and Gawain reigniting the Sacred Band, the tale of the quest for the Grail, the arrival at Thebes and the ruined Citadel of Cadmea. The fragments of stories his father had told him while he was growing up and during training, since he was the brother born to the Band, sadly Luke appearing not to be the chosen one. William Wood and his family must have experienced the same through the generations, brothers born one for the Band, the other for the Blade. In this instance, William became the Knight of Gawain, while his brother Chris belonged to the Sacred Band. His brother Luke was now destined not to bear his father's own sword, following its destruction by Mary as Athena incarnate, but Excalibur a worthy replacement… if he could manage to wield it.

'Is there another *Allen* on that list Fernando?' Adam asked.

'Err, yessir, but I couldn't reach him,' Fernando said. 'So sorry.'

Luke snapped his glare back to his brother. 'Uncle Alex? You think it's Uncle Alex? Dad's *brother*?'

'Would make sense,' Adam drily replied.

'I thought he was dead? Died on active duty during the Gulf War or something?' Luke was blunt.

'Suffered from some form of post-traumatic stress and retired shortly after the conflict. He didn't die, although Mum and Dad did occasionally say of him that he would rather have.' Adam pursed his lips.

'We ever meet him?' Luke asked.

'Maybe when young. Like William with his brother Chris, I doubt Dad ever got him over the line. Hardly ever spoke of him. Not sure they stayed in touch,' Adam replied, piecing together why their father Richard spent every hour he could raising him as a Sacred Band, in contrast with his apparent failure with his brother.

'Was he gay?' Luke kept hammering out his questions.

'I really don't know, Luke.' Adam tired.

'So, what are we going to do now?' Aisha wondered. Gary turned and squarely approached Fernando.

'How soon can these guys you've rallied get to Mount Sinai?'

CHAPTER 19

━━━▶◆◀━━━

ALEXANDRIA, EGYPT

2nd June 2012 AD

A FEW CHEERS HAD COME FROM ACROSS THE FAR SIDE OF THE BAR, followed by chants of victory. The rowdy group was mostly made up of students, always the most vocal during elections, and always with the most to lose, Sir Lawrence thought to himself as he sat quietly in the corner peeking up over the top of the local newspaper. The next generation, passionate if sometimes a little short-sighted when it came to change, he sighed.

He slapped his neck instinctively upon feeling the nip of a mosquito and muttered a curse word or two – that was the third one since he had sat down. He'd put off returning to Egypt as long as he could, despite political pressures, agreeing with his government to only make an appearance at the end of the country's first round of voting. He could make plenty of excuses for the delay – political instability of the region, the lighter touch of diplomacy and so on, but the truth was he just couldn't stand the sweltering heat of the place, and it wasn't even the cruel part of the summer yet. He grumbled to himself while waving to the young barman for another whisky.

The calendar on his phone came to life. Eleven days until the transit of Venus, if Geraint South was to be believed. Less than two weeks and this will all be over, just the idea enough to let Sir Lawrence unwind his muscles as if relaxed by a tonic. Soothing to think that he and Lady Morgan could finally be together as one, in a land where they made the rules. A destiny fulfilled, unlike any of his ancestors before him. Where they had failed, he would succeed.

The whisky was placed by his side accompanied by a timid smile from the young barman. Fresh-faced, olive-skinned, the shadow of a first beard beginning to show. What would someone like him inherit, Sir Lawrence wondered. Would he and Lady Morgan have a place for him? What would he believe in? Would people merely follow as they have always done, or would they rebel like their enemies in the Red Dragon? Blind loyalty… it has its uses, provided it can be controlled. A sip of whisky caught in his throat, Sir Lawrence coughed and dribbled, setting the glass down quickly. A white handkerchief dabbed the spots away from his crisp green tie, Morgan's favourite. Sir Lawrence cursed privately again. This past month he'd sensed the growing distraction from his wife, rarely speaking of anything other than her own obsessions, often choosing to say nothing to him at all – understandable perhaps, he tried to soothe himself. Despite knowing Lady Morgan so long and sharing a purpose, he knew enough to be able to discipline his emotions. This was no ordinary marriage, it was never meant to be. Whatever feelings he held for his wife, they were to be cast aside, *sacrificed* if you will, for something far greater.

'Am I disturbing?' Geraint South pulled up a chair.

'Nearly always.' Sir Lawrence grunted, ruffling his paper. 'I can only assume you are here to tell me that something has gone wrong back in England? That despite all the firepower of Mr Hussin's men, the ruthlessness of the followers to Palamedes, and the Allen brothers trapped like cornered rats in a hospital in Cardiff, we still don't have Excalibur?' he growled.

Geraint fidgeted in his tweed jacket. 'Not quite, sir. Please, one moment… my phone.'

'If that's Lady Morgan, I'd rather not know, if it's all the same to you. I am getting sick of hearing my wife's news through others!' Sir Lawrence snapped. Geraint offered an ill-timed look of sympathy, retracting it immediately. He fumbled his fingers over his phone and revealed a message.

'Here, sir. From, well, your wife. We must go to Mount Sinai and the Monastery of Saint Catherine, immediately.' Geraint stuttered. 'It's as we said, the connection to Hypatia and the transit of Venus. Her desire to awaken the Old Ways and the spirits of...'

'Yes, Geraint. Yes... you've told me.' Sir Lawrence studied the message from Lady Morgan. It was brief, a terse order followed by the familiar *Albus Draco*. They were to travel to the monastery, just them, no soldiers or guns for hire, no back-up of any kind. It made Sir Lawrence feel uneasy, too exposed to failure at the most crucial of times. 'Mohammed Hussin, he too has received this message?' he asked.

'Yes, I believe so.'

'And he is to come alone? No fighters of his own?' Sir Lawrence continued. Geraint could only shrug. 'Does he have Excalibur?'

'Well, no, not exactly, Sir Lawrence.' Geraint gazed at the floor. Sir Lawrence leaned in.

'What do you mean... *not exactly*?' came a sneer.

'I mean, the Red Dragon have said they will present Excalibur to us. On the very day of the transit.' Geraint stuttered. Sir Lawrence sat upright.

'Why? That makes no sense,' he said aloud to himself. 'What sort of trick are they playing?'

South breathed a sigh of relief at retrieving some space from Sir Lawrence. 'Perhaps they've given in? Maybe the notion of working with us in the White Dragon as one has finally won them over?' he chirped. 'With both Mr Richard Allen and Mr William Wood now gone, perhaps they're leaderless?'

'Not with Richard's sons still alive. Do not underestimate them, especially a Sacred Band member,' Sir Lawrence cautioned. 'What of the efforts of Mr Hussin in Cardiff?'

'We know Nick Butcher, son of Sir Bors, fell at The Blue Hare pub in the assault. There were two other bodies. One was of a Mr Carl Bishop, a journalist for the *York Post* and allied to Gary Willis, son of Sir Gaheris. The other one, we're not sure. Their support grows thin, Sir Lawrence,' Geraint reassured.

'There's still the Sacred Band. As dispersed as it is, they put on a formidable show in Edinburgh, and that was a mere handful. I do not relish the thought of three hundred of them showing up when we are all but defenceless.' Sir Lawrence took a large gulp of his whisky.

'But will we have the Trinity, sir? Surely when it's in the hands of Lady Morgan, all else will be rendered inert?' Geraint proclaimed. Sir Lawrence shot another fierce glance his way.

'Have Mr Hussin assemble and bring his men to Mount Sinai ready for the fourth of June,' Sir Lawrence snapped.

'But Sir Lawrence… Lady Morgan said only to…'

'I don't care what Lady Morgan said. Give the order!' Sir Lawrence snapped again.

'Very well, sir. But I know Mr Hussin has been given another task to perform by Lady Morgan,' Geraint sheepishly replied.

'What? What order?'

'To collect his wife, Mrs Ahmal Hussin. I say *collect*, just bring with us apparently,' Geraint explained. Sir Lawrence's eyes narrowed, confusion getting the better of his anger. Why bring his wife? What would be the purpose of bringing her into this, now of all times? He screwed his eyes tight shut, subduing his rage over yet more insubordination, then emptied his lungs in submission.

'Fine. Just please give *my order*, Geraint.'

CHAPTER 20

SHARM EL-SHEIKH, EGYPT
3rd June 2012 AD

M*ORE SAND*, ADAM THOUGHT. OCEANS OF THE SUBSTANCE, stretching far into the horizon, ripe ginger in colour and shimmering in the midday summer heat. He'd caught little sleep on the plane, tossing and turning in the narrow economy class seat next to Luke, who managed to snore his way through any situation the world threw at him, at a volume close to the rumble of the jet engines, mouth slack and open. Violet occasionally amused herself by laying paper napkins over his mouth to see how high he could blow them.

Gary had spent much of the journey seated behind the two, liaising endlessly with Fernando, grilling the young Italian on every detail when it came to the Sacred Band contacts. How many? How certain? Rarely did the answers give him the reassurance he craved, causing him to fidget more and more with the back of Adam's chair as the flight dragged on. Truth was, there was little any of them could do now but wait. The die had been cast the moment Gary issued word to the White Dragon, through familiar lines in the press, knowing Geraint South would likely pick it up. No more than a few hours later, the accord had been reached.

'We'll be spotted. I know we'll be spotted,' Aisha said when the wheels touched down on the runway tarmac. 'My father will see to it that we are.' She twitched nervously.

'Almost certainly. Still, that's kind of what we want,' Adam reassured.

'You certain of all this?' Aisha asked.

'Not in the slightest. But then I haven't been certain of much, lately,' Adam confessed.

Standing in a bustling taxi rank with drivers touting for business, Fernando put a flat palm to his forehead and peered through the heat haze. 'Sir Gary, sir. I think that... that gentleman over there, that might be a contact,' he stuttered. Gary cocked his head to one side to try and make out the relatively slender shape of the man in a headscarf and casual khaki clothing. Although not immediately familiar, his presence mirrored that of a comforting friend. *William Wood,* Gary thought instantly... same posture, same reassuring sense of confidence even when evidently a fish out of water.

'Mr Willis, it's been some time,' Chris Wood stretched out a welcoming hand, 'and for that I must apologise.' He removed his tinted glasses to reveal his brother's cut-glass eyes. His mature muscles were bunched, tensing with every word as he scouted in all directions.

❧

'Afraid I can't recall the last time we met Chris. Been somewhat of a loose end of late,' Gary quipped. 'I take it you know about your brother William?' Chris nodded, still distracted.

'I wanted to reach out, truly I did. For so long I tried but...' Chris snapped his glare across Gary's shoulder into the crowds behind. 'I'm being *watched.* Have been since London.'

'Might want to get used to that, pal,' Luke snorted while rummaging through his side bag for the short wooden staff of Excalibur. 'Think you'll find they're looking for this.' Adam immediately moved to shroud the item from view.

'We can't stay here. Too risky.' Chris muttered, already taking steps towards the nearest cab. 'I suggest we make our way to the hotel I booked just down the road, we can regroup there.'

Aisha gave an incredulous look. 'You really think my father won't know you're here… that we're all here? His men practically run this part of the Middle East! Trust me, I know how far his connections go.' Wood froze upon hearing her words and tightened his fist to spark blue flame.

'And who exactly are you?' Chris's tone deepened with suspicion.

'It's OK, she's with us.' Adam soothed his fellow Sacred Band member until the fire fizzled out.

'How so?' Chris sneered, unconvinced.

'Well, if you'd bothered to be around for the past decade, Chris, to help your brother and Karen, you might be more in tune.' Gary dealt a low blow.

Chris pinched his brow. 'This was a mistake. I should never have left London – gotten pulled back into all William's nonsense again. Sick of it. Of all of you!' he blurted and hailed another cab, only to have Fernando seize his wrist.

'Please, sir, Mr Wood. We spoke earlier. I am Fernando Russo. Friend of Mr Graham McCreedy, yes?' Fernando soothed.

'McCreedy. Yes, that old bugger. I know, I know. You going to tell me he's dead too right?' Chris sparked. Fernando's mournful face was his answer. 'I'm… I'm sorry. You didn't say anything in your message. I… well, let's just say this is I what I wanted to avoid. No good can come from this life.' He sighed.

'So he died for *nothing?*' Fernando produced an uncharacteristic flash of rage. Wood tipped his face to the skies and exhaled heavily.

'Look, it's only me, OK. I have no partner, no warrior teammate of any kind. I'm limited in my fighting skills and not sure I'll be much use to you,' Chris confessed.

'Then why come?' Adam shot back.

'You must be Richard's son. You've certainly grown. Look more like your mother, mind,' Chris replied flippantly. 'I'm sure Richard prepared you and your partner for battle, but I'm a stockbroker, not a hoplite.'

'I don't have *a partner* either.' Adam stood firm. 'And if you can summon your shield like you were clearly about to, then you are of value, no matter what training you think you should have had or believe you might have missed in your youth.' His focus came as a surprise to none more than himself.

Chris scratched his neck awkwardly, turned and hissed under his breath 'This is madness' before composing himself. 'Fine. What do you have in mind? Please tell me it's not just the seven of us against all of the White Dragon?' he replied.

'I have spoken with other Sacred Band members, sir. Friends of Mr McCreedy.' Fernando confirmed.

'And?'

'And... well, they said they would come. Help us fight.'

'And you believed them?' Chris tutted in disbelief. Fernando looked wounded once more. 'You're kidding yourself, boy.'

'You showed up,' Adam affirmed.

'I had reason to. Because of Bill, and Karen...' Chris protested in response. 'Others like us won't fight. Maybe a few but not enough.'

'We thought that in Edinburgh. Perhaps the others have just as much to lose as you do,' Adam pushed back.

Chris bowed his head, recalling the newspaper headline from earlier in the year depicting the unusual display of the Northern Lights over the Scottish capital, together with an ignored message from Graham McCreedy for help. The combination of all these factors lent credence to Wood's true reason for arriving in Egypt now. He couldn't let his brother down once again. 'Same blind sense of duty. Let nobody doubt you are Richard Allen's son.' Chris cracked a smile.

There was a jolt from Aisha, Luke felt it, followed by the distinctive click of a gun. 'Forgive the intrusion, Miss Hussin. Your father, Mohammed Hussin, would care for a word with you and your friends,' came a coarse and commanding tone from behind them. More clicks rattled the group, figures of shadow and white cloth forming a tight circle around them.

'Check,' Violet whispered to Luke.

CHAPTER 21

⋙◆⋘

MOUNT SINAI, EGYPT

4th June 2012 AD

'ARE YOU DISPLEASED WITH ME?' SIR LAWRENCE ASKED, drawing close to his wife. Her lily-white arm was bare, arousing him as it glistened in the morning sun. His instinct was to touch it, a reminder of the feeling of his own skin against hers, but he couldn't bring himself to, as if such an act would expose a weakness that would make her cast him from her side in utmost disgust. He clamped his hands behind his back and squared his shoulders resolutely.

'It matters not, now, my love. If conjuring up the soldiers of Palamedes reassures you, then so be it,' Lady Morgan replied firmly. Sir Lawrence had over the years grown accustomed to her sternness, seen as a source of strength by all those that had unquestioningly followed her for all these generations. For Sir Lawrence, though, there was always an unspoken bond between Lady Morgan and the Knights of Lancelot, a closeness that was never shared with the other knights of the White Dragon. For this, he always felt privileged. Of late, it was as if that unique connection had frayed, worn away at by a blinkered vision so twisted that their love for one another had been stripped away. Reduced to an unnecessary distraction or at best, an

109

inconvenience. Sir Lawrence had always accepted his place as head of White Dragon, leader of the men and the one true *Chevalier Blanc,* or *White Knight* in the Anglo-Saxon tongue. For all such posturing, he was still cowering in his wife's shadow, as all his ancestors had done before him. His father once stated that *"while men may follow their women into battle, never should they stand by their side."* More of a cautionary tale of patriarchal preservation, he later came to understand, punctuating his thoughts with scenes of Boudicca and Joan of Arc over the long centuries. Envy would creep in each time, figures renowned for commanding respect without need of Arthurian lineage, swords or magical statues, all meeting a grizzly end, but perhaps a more precious legacy than what his kin had managed to accomplish.

Sir Lawrence caught the soft mewing sound of Ahmal Hussin. She pleaded with the three guards rooted in front of her, fingers itching on their triggers. 'May I ask Morgan the purpose of Mohammed Hussin bringing his wife to join us on this most auspicious of occasions?' he asked calmly.

Lady Morgan's gaze remained fixed on the horizon and the track of dust thrown up by the approaching 4x4 vehicles. 'Truly remarkable that after all my years upon this very earth, my sister still manages to surprise me. I thought I'd seen sacrifice in every conceivable form. Turns out I have not,' she murmured.

Violet gulped hard as she stepped out of the jeep, immediately scanning the rugged terrain and counting the number of pin-sized hooded figures atop each peak. They were certainly outnumbered. She huddled into Luke while whispering to Aisha, 'These all your dad's guys?' Aisha gave a quick nod before being ordered by the guard behind her to make for the monastery, his rifle butt pressing into the small of her back.

'This all part of the plan?' Chris Wood leaned into Gary hesitantly. 'Might want to think about using that *walking stick* of yours soon.' He gestured to Willis's staff. Gary ignored him and turned to Fernando, his expression hopeful of good news on any Sacred Band reinforcements heading their way. Fernando shook his head with a timid shrug. There was no one else at the site.

'Friends of the Red Dragon, I bid you welcome,' Lady Morgan gushed. 'While you are now few in number, save the Knights of Sir Gaheris, you come to witness your true destiny. A return to the Old Ways, a world reborn.' Her arms stretched out theatrically. 'Master Luke Allen, I trust you have brought what was agreed?'

Luke opened his side satchel and revealed the carved wooden hilt of Excalibur. Lady Morgan struggled to retain her composure, her excitement betrayed by a sharp intake of breath. She brought her hands together in mock prayer. 'Extraordinary. Truly extraordinary. Your father Richard would be so proud. If only he were alive to see what we are about to accomplish together,' she purred.

Adam twisted his jaw in agitation upon hearing the sorceress mention his father's name. Narrowing his eyes, his anger was broken by a scream from Aisha.

'Mother! Mother!' she cried, taking two steps towards Ahmal before she was brutally wrestled away by the muscular arm of a guard. 'Why is she here?' Why!' Aisha demanded.

'Oh my child, you'll soon see. Such desire and passion I see in you, just like your own father, our trusted Mohammed Hussin.' Lady Morgan answered. 'The loyalty of men can be bought for so little now... Let us change that notion, shall we?' She swept her arm to display the soldiers of Palamedes. 'Come, the transit is soon upon us.' She led the way up the cobbled footpath to the summit of Mount Sinai.

The soldiers flanked the group as they stumbled up the dusty path to the top. The rising sun scorched the air, and Violet occasionally stopped to cough while resting her weight on her father's staff. Adam offered his hand in support, but it was stoically rejected. Sir Lawrence dropped back to Gary. 'Change of heart, Sir Gaheris?' he snipped. Gary remained silent. 'I am sorry about Richard Allen, and William

Wood, for all your fellow Red Dragon followers for that matter. I trust you know that?' he offered a shred of decency.

'My brother. You murdered him!' Chris spat across Gary, teeth gritted.

'Not what I recall,' Sir Lawrence retorted. 'I'm sure Mr Willis and the Allen Brothers here can recount the events of Edinburgh just fine.'

'You tried to murder *me*,' Violet corrected, pushing her way to confront the gaunt frame of Sir Lawrence, lower lip protruding. 'And that son of a bitch Mr Hussin and his thugs took my dad.' The lip now started to quiver. Sir Lawrence as always seemingly unperturbed.

'You have my condolences as well, Miss Violet, daughter of Sir Bors. I see you have taken up the mantle quite nicely, however.' He pointed to her staff. 'What a future you have in store for you.'

The summit drew near and Aisha could make out the imposing figure of her father standing, staff on one side, the weaselly shape of Geraint South to the other. She tried to scream out to him but her lungs were spent from the climb, she could only fall to her knees, fingertips crawling across the hot stones towards her mother just as Ahmal was dragged before Lady Morgan.

'It would be remiss if I did not pay tribute to the visionary that was Hypatia, a true follower of the Old Ways and defender of the real faith, faith in Mother Earth itself,' Lady Morgan declaimed over the tears and cries of Ahmal and Aisha. 'Our Saint Catherine, as she became known, canonised by the very church that saw fit to butcher her, still revered to this day. And now, upon the mount where she was killed, and with the light of the Morning Star in transit, I seek permission to bring forth the *Trinity*. The basis for all belief in this world, and the foundations of the Old Ways, *reborn,*' she concluded, with a nod to Mr Hussin. 'Mohammed, if you please.'

Hussin stepped forward with the Palladium, pristine and intricate, as if just carved by the finest sculptor only moments ago. Luke shuddered as the statue exchanged hands and was clutched by Lady Morgan. The subdued Necklace around her throat immediately pulsed into life, the ruby-red glow like a smouldering ember framed in fine gold.

'The Palladium of Pallas Athena… founder of empires, the *birth*.' Lady Morgan held the statue aloft. 'Together with the Necklace of Harmonia… desire and lust, the embodiment of *life*.' She touched the jewel delicately, then cast her eyes upon Luke.

'And finally, from the bloodline of our dearest companion, the Knights of Sir Galahad, in service to King Arthur Pendragon. The king's blade… Excalibur. The sword of *death*.' Lady Morgan's tone softened in trepidation. Luke drew a deep breath and pulled the staff from the satchel once more. He stepped forward and presented the polished end to the frosty fingertips of Lady Morgan. There was a second of hesitation, no doubt wary of her previous encounter with the blade, Adam thought, but she swiftly seized it with an almost juvenile chortle of disbelief. The Trinity was *hers*. She straightened, the Palladium lowered in one hand, Excalibur in the other, the Necklace casting enough light now to cause Adam to squint. She beckoned the guard who was restraining Ahmal, had him hold her in front of her husband, then commanded that Aisha be held by her side. Mr Hussin recoiled in horror as Lady Morgan hissed the words 'Choose – Knight of Palamedes.'

CHAPTER 22

MOUNT SINAI, EGYPT

4th June 2012 AD

'MORGAN, ENOUGH OF THIS MADNESS!' GARY STRAINED WILDLY against his guard's restraint, his staff out of reach in the hands of another. 'You have what you want. The Trinity. Perform whatever it is you want and be done with us,' he continued his outburst. Lady Morgan maintained her silence. 'Lawrence. Is this what you have been reduced to by this hag? The slaughter of two innocents? This is your New World Order?'

'Incorrect, Knight of Sir Gaheris. It is not slaughter,' Lady Morgan interjected. 'Mr Hussin, I bid you again, choose. Or all three of you die.' Hussin tried to clear the shock from his face, his own staff trembling in his hand, sweat cresting the knuckles. His daughter was pleading with him to choose her, his wife had locked her arms around Aisha's head protectively. Adam, Luke, Violet and Chris stared, unable to speak. Geraint South rocked uncomfortably on his heels in an attempt to disassociate himself from the unfolding events. Sir Lawrence uncharacteristically twitched his right eyebrow in modest disapproval. 'Time is slipping, Mohammed, don't make me choose for you,' Lady Morgan chimed in again.

A fleeting last look from Ahmal as she mouthed what Adam took as forgiveness, followed by a sharp execution by Hussin's sword. A spray of blood peppered the sky, drowning out any sound from Aisha's lips as her mother fell neatly to the ground. Hussin could only stare at his wife's warm corpse, his concentration not broken even by the delayed shriek of anguish from his daughter, as she collapsed by her mother's side, sobbing.

'Of course, you chose your wife. What better sacrifice can this world witness than a mother's life for her daughter's?' Lady Morgan spoke once more. 'I have witnessed sacrifice so many times over my life, but none so poignant as this. It took my sister's knowledge, a servant of Mother Earth, to understand this power, the power of the feminine beyond the masculine. Not William Wood, not a Sacred Band brother, not even the Father that was King Arthur, but the Mother for the Child. I have witnessed it. Finally, I, Morgan le Fay, now *understand.*' She cackled as thunder crashed and lightning raged above the mount.

'No. No, you *don't,* Morgan.' Luke's voice cut like crystal as he broke ranks to rush to Aisha's side.

'Silence! This world shall come to follow me once more, not the would-be lords of false deities. All faiths shall bow to mine, the spirit and essence of the Earth as it should be,' Lady Morgan proclaimed.

Luke smiled at his brother Adam, who was looking perplexed. 'I don't see Excalibur in your hands, Lady Morgan, I see a wooden pole,' he mocked. Adam did a double-take. Despite the grand light show occurring over their heads, Excalibur had not yet revealed itself in its true form, despite being in the presence of the Palladium and Necklace of Harmonia for the first time. Surely now? What was stopping the great sorceress?

Luke pulled a still sobbing Aisha to her feet and landed a kiss on her cheek. 'I'm sorry Aisha, for your mother, I truly am – this bastard took ours too,' he comforted her. 'But your father will never wield that sword, nor will Lady Morgan.'

'What are you on about, boy?' Geraint South protested. 'This is Morgan le Fay, the spirit of the Earth and sister to the Lady of the Lake. She has fulfilled her prophecy of wielding the Trinity, having witnessed true sacrifice under the transit of the most sacred planet of womanhood and...' he tripped over his own words frantically.

'And yet she doesn't love anything more than *herself*,' Luke cut him off. 'And Excalibur *knows* it.' He paused to take stock and look once more at Adam. 'That's *true* sacrifice. Sorry, bro.' Adam already knew deep down inside, had known for some time, he just didn't want to admit it. He wasn't ready to say the words until now. Iain Donnelly didn't love him above all else. Excalibur could thus never be in his partner's hands either.

Sir Lawrence stood solemnly by Lady Morgan's side. He ventured a hand of comfort to his wife, but refrained when he caught her chilling gaze. Muttering in a language even he could not decipher, shaking Excalibur in frustration, she finally spewed accursed words his direction. 'Kill them all.' He flared his broad nostrils at the order and started to counter. *'Kill them all!'* Lady Morgan bellowed.

CHAPTER 23

MOUNT SINAI, EGYPT

4th June 2012 AD

THE MORNING SKIES HAD DARKENED IN AN INSTANT. MR HUSSIN'S mouth was still parched, in shock at his actions, rasping out an order to his men to slay all Red Dragon followers. Before any gun muzzles could be raised, Gary and Chris had read the move and got free of their captors – Gary landing his elbow sharply into the ribs of the soldier behind him, Chris opting to try and wrestle the rifle away from his captor in a moment of adrenaline-fuelled panic. Wood was forced to the ground, overpowered by his bulky opponent, but caught the edge of Gary's confiscated staff with his boot and flicked it across to Willis. 'Gary!' he cried as the staff rattled over the stones. Gary rolled away nimbly and seized the handle, swinging it ferociously towards the still winded soldier, knocking him out cold. Fernando took advantage of the commotion by hauling up the nearest rock he could find and bringing it down heavily onto the skull of the brute that pinned down Chris. Wood heaved a breath of relief. Then the rain of bullets from above began, forcing Gary and Fernando to seek cover under Chris's blue shield. 'I can't hold this!' Wood groaned.

A streak of blue fire flared from Adam's hand, bringing down two Palamedes gunmen from their vantage points above. A brief reprieve for the three as Gary found cover in an alcove. He turned back quickly to see Adam summon a second spear, this one missing its targets but prompting several soldiers to retreat. One of Sir Lawrence's blades cut the air above Adam's head as he ducked, his shield blocking the other as Worthington spun on his heel, letting out a blood-curdling roar. The two men locked in combat on the edge of the cliff.

Luke instinctively bolted for Lady Morgan and Excalibur, being marked by Geraint. South's sword revealed itself with a glint, but the knight hacked the air furiously with little control. Luke fell on to his back, appearing to concede to South, but landed a solid kick to the kneecap of the squat Geraint, causing him to squeal out in pain. Violet charged South like a wild animal, locking her small arm around his neck and pulling him to the ground. Luke finished the job with a hard punch to his jaw. 'Thanks... but this is where you run and hide, Violet.' Luke sheltered her as best he could under his torso. Her eyes looked over his shoulder, fear-stricken. She forced her way on top of him with a strength that surprised Luke, brought her father's staff to the fore and tensed her face in concentration. The single spark of a successfully deflected bullet flashed upon the sword blade now in her hand. Luke's expression turned from relieved to quizzical as Violet admired the weapon she now commanded. 'Fine – stay on the front line, daughter of Sir Bors,' he smiled.

'Father, enough. Look what you are doing.' Aisha ran to Hussin, her plea quickly turning to anger. 'You're not a monster. But you've let one corrupt you.' She tugged his arm urgently. 'Lady Morgan, the White Dragon... all of this. This isn't who you are,' she burst out. Mohammed's stone composure began to break, his glare darting between his daughter and Lady Morgan. He took another fleeting look down at the body of his wife Ahmal, her blood pooling by his feet. The next moment, he yelled 'For Palamedes!' and threw himself and his sword directly at the sorceress. The blade glanced down by Lady Morgan's side as she sidestepped it, Hussin swinging again.

'Witch!' he cried. Lady Morgan's eyes blazed green. The third swing of his sword was effortlessly caught in her hand.

'Such a disappointment, Mr Hussin,' Lady Morgan sighed against the grimace of Mohammed as he tried to force his blade closer. A snap of bright green light shot through Mr Hussin's body, causing him to convulse, then lifelessly he fell from the cliff. Aisha let out a scream. 'Would you care to try instead, young knight of Palamedes?' Lady Morgan teased Aisha, still holding her father's sword by the tip. 'Perhaps a woman can do a man's job?' she cackled.

'Aisha! No!' Luke ran between the two, his pistol firing off several rounds, which just bounced off Lady Morgan. 'You're going to have to go through me, bitch,' he swore.

'Wouldn't have it any other way, Master Allen,' Lady Morgan grinned. A streak of green pierced Luke in the midriff, bringing him down to his knees with a whelp. 'Just like Richard. All action, no thought,' she mocked.

'And he's all the better for it,' came the biting remark from Violet as she vaulted from behind Lady Morgan, her sword held high. The sorceress was forced to turn to deflect the blow, repulsing Violet's small body back against the rocks. It was enough to expose her hand, which was still holding Excalibur. Luke took his chance and gripped Lady Morgan's wrist, wedging his fingers beneath her grip on the hilt just enough to twist it at his will. The tip pierced Lady Morgan's thigh, she winced in pain and began to relinquish her hold on the sword. Luke heaved and wrenched Excalibur free from her grasp. Aisha watched him stumble back and realised that the witch, to stanch the blood spurting from her wound, had dropped her father's sword.

A shower of blue sparks appeared each time Adam raised a defence against Sir Lawrence's attacks. No sooner had he conjured up his shield of blue fire against one of Worthington's blades than Sir Lawrence pressed forward, possessed, forcing Adam to retreat. Each thrust came with more vigour, his grey fringe matted with sweat, skin mottled red from the exertion. 'Your father tried to deny me. Deny *us*. Time and time again, Adam. And for what? The legacy of a weak king? The extinction of our own beliefs?' Sir Lawrence sneered with whatever breath he had left in him. Adam quickly got a heel to his gaunt opponent's shoulder, pushing him back from the cliff edge. He followed with a low punch to the groin, then managed to swerve away from Worthington's first sword, but not the second. The slash across Adam's chest stung, and he hurled a spear in Sir Lawrence's direction, but it missed and sailed over his head. All Adam could do was bring a final shield up in desperation as another sword edge came whistling down. The shield did not hold, and he collapsed onto his back, clutching his forearm, grinding his teeth in pain.

'You were offered the chance, young Mr Allen. So was your father. All of the Red Dragon... time and time again.' Sir Lawrence puffed, bringing the point of a sword to Adam's throat. 'Morgan tried to help you, your kind. The Sacred Band – a brotherhood of courage and allegiance, persecuted in this time for who they are. She can change that. Why fight what we believe in?'

Adam held Sir Lawrence's gaze as he chose his response carefully. 'Because it's not what I believe in, Larry. Nor should it be what you, or Lady Morgan, believe in.' He levered himself up to his feet. 'It's... not... about... *you*.'

Sir Lawrence allowed Adam's defiance. The shiver passed down his arm right through to his sword. 'You're quite correct, Adam. My wife has taught me that.'

'And you believe you'll rule by her side, Sir Lawrence? As what? A king? Like she promised Mordred all those years ago?' Adam reminded him. 'You'll never be her equal.'

'I don't have to be.'

'Yes, you do. What else is a partnership if not of equals? And for that, you need the one thing Lady Morgan can't give you.'

Sir Lawrence's left eye twitched. He tried to shake it off. 'Which is...?'

'You know what it is, Larry. The same thing Iain Donnelly denied me. She doesn't love you more than she…' Adam was thrown to the ground by an enraged Sir Lawrence, blade pressed against his throat.

'It's… not… true!' Sir Lawrence hissed. Adam drew in what air he could, feeling the cold metal slice deeper into his throat.

'I'm sorry, Sir Lawrence. You can't argue with the king's blade, you know that.' Adam choked. He felt the pressure ease and dared open his eyes to see Sir Lawrence throw one of his swords straight behind him. It met its target, Lady Morgan's shoulder. A spray of green light blinded Luke and Violet, her scream echoed across the mountain. Aisha fumbled at her feet to retrieve Hussin's staff, catching sight of the Palladium, that had been left upon a low mound of rocks, unguarded.

CHAPTER 24

---◆---

MOUNT SINAI, EGYPT

4ᵗʰ June 2012 AD

'THE WEAKNESS OF MEN ONCE MORE,' LADY MORGAN TUTTED, removing Sir Lawrence's sword with a careless groan. 'Am I forever to be cursed with your king's failure?' She brought a palm to the beam of light emitted from her pierced skin. The mark faded almost as quickly as it was made. Luke rallied, managing to lift Excalibur to chest height, only to be thrown back in a pulse of green energy. 'Very well.' Her hands were spread, hovering inches above the ground. She murmured in an unknown tongue, the gravel and stones shaking all around her. As she lifted her hands, the very earth itself replied with a voice of its own.

Gary ushered Chris and Fernando clear of the alcove. 'Go, go. She's bringing down the whole mountain!' he yelled. The soldiers ceased their fire and scrambled for firm ground, many swallowed by the chasms splitting beneath their feet. Aisha crawled behind Lady Morgan on all fours, reaching out to the Palladium. It tilted her way, only to shift to its side and tumble farther away as the tremors grew stronger. She stretched, sliding her father's staff through her hands like a snooker cue. The statue flicked up and rolled along the wood into her hands. 'Luke!' she cried out. He caught her eye just as the cliff broke away underneath her feet.

'Aisha! No!' Luke sprinted, clutched her loose sleeve. She dangled hopelessly for a moment, Luke throwing all his weight back in counterbalance, until Violet darted over to grab her other arm. 'Pull!'

The remaining gunmen opened fire in all directions as solid lumps of rock merged to form giant, faceless golems. Their sounds, like the rumble of the avalanches that created them, boomed through their ears. Bullets ricocheted around Geraint South as he whimpered his way across to Sir Lawrence. 'Sir. Please… we're all going to die,' he begged. A boulder the size of a truck flew through the sky in their direction, and Sir Lawrence wrapped his body across Geraint's, throwing the two clear of its path.

'Not just yet, Sir Geraint.' Sir Lawrence breathed heavily while lying on top of the smaller knight. 'For now, let's stand as one and end this. Help Sir Gaheris,' he ordered.

'Sir?'

'I said *help him*. Help Gary Willis,' Sir Lawrence ordered again, finding his feet.

Chris Wood held his shield aloft to protect Fernando. Lone soldiers were still firing at the stone beasts to no avail. 'Nothing works against these creatures, Gary,' he shouted across to his companion just as Willis drove his sword into the ground to cast a shimmering white knight light, prompting a modest retreat of the nearest golem, but not significant enough. 'We need more. More firepower.' The three huddled together as the golem towered above them, its fists casting a shadow. Electric blue then lit up the air around them. The familiar chant *'We… are… Lions!'* came from the clouds of dust and smoke behind.

'Think we just got our firepower, sirs.' Fernando smiled. A neat line of blue fire capped the nearby ridge, he guessed sixty to seventy strong at least. *'They came.'*

'Destroy them!' Lady Morgan screeched. Her stone pawns turned their attention to the army of Sacred Band warriors. Blue spears whistled across, causing a flurry of explosions upon impact. Two of the three golems fell, to cheers from the Band, the third crashing through the front line of shields to the right flank, sending men tree-high into the air.

'Adam. That Band is leaderless. Go and assist them,' Gary shouted, watching the two fallen golems reform in a matter of minutes. 'Chris, go with him. Help hold the line.'

'We can't stop them, Gary,' Chris confessed.

'No, but you can buy us time,' Gary replied. 'Go.'

Adam grabbed Chris by the scruff of his neck and positioned him next to the strikers for Celtic FC. 'Stay with these two – shield up,' he commanded. 'The rest of you, with me. Keep these bastards distracted. Spears!' Another volley of blue showered across, one golem falling again. A boulder was flung in response, scattering several Band members. 'Cover!' Adam yelled to those still standing. He looked across at his brother Luke, standing close to Violet and still aiding Aisha back to safe ground. They did need more time, and if one of these monsters turned about at Lady Morgan's request, it was over. They needed to cut them off – drive a wedge between them and their master.

'Battle of Leuctra,' he muttered.

'What?' Chris moaned, wiping a head wound with the tail of his shirt.

'The Battle of Leuctra – 371 BC. One of the few times the Spartans lost.' Adam mused further. 'The Sacred Band engaged the weaker flank, came from the left side and forced them apart. Ugly and unusual tactic for the time, but it was successful.'

'Ugly and unusual is likely all we've got.' Chris spat while ducking for cover from the fragments sprayed out from a landing boulder. 'You think any of those good-for-little gunmen can help us out?' he pointed to the hooded soldiers making for the distant hills.

Adam looked at them despondently, then a thought appeared. 'Aisha. They are followers of Palamedes, so Aisha is their leader now,' he realised while climbing a nearby rocky outcrop. He signalled over to his brother and Violet. 'Come on Miss Hussin – time to go to work.'

'What's he saying?' Violet tugged on Luke's arm as he cradled Aisha. 'Adam. He's trying to tell us something.' Luke was preoccupied with Aisha, unwilling to release his hold, having come so close to losing her. His prize wriggled free and stood stridently between him and Violet. 'I'm needed,' she barked with newfound confidence. 'Here – you two, take care of this.' She thrust the Palladium into Luke's hands. 'Send that witch back to hell.' Her father's sword raised, she bellowed out 'For Palamedes!' with a fervour that made both Luke and Violet jump in fright. Her men paused to absorb her cry, looked at each other briefly before turning about and raining bullets back on each golem.

'Can't say I saw that coming,' Luke admitted frankly.

'You heard her, Luke.' Violet pointed to Excalibur in his hand, then to the Palladium in the other. 'Check.' She cracked a grin.

'Now, we need checkmate,' he riposted.

CHAPTER 25

MOUNT SINAI, EGYPT

4th June 2012 AD

LIKE THE SANDS THAT SHIFTED AROUND HER, LADY MORGAN knew her time was running out. The transit of Venus was peaking, and within minutes her newly forged strength would ebb away, her control of the Earth with it. She felt renewed, as if clean for the first time after many years, her skin delicate and rejuvenated. Even if the ritual of the Trinity could not be completed by her hand, faiths were undone at the mercy of her own, she could make a mark upon this world so profound she would ensure her survival. The Old Ways would be heard and feared by men once more. The chance was hers to seize.

The young Allen boy's move had successfully cut off two of her mighty golems, his Sacred Band forming the blue wall of old and frantically throwing spears of flame into their stony backs. While fire would never conquer rock, she thought, the blood-red face of her husband charging ever closer, a bitter expression showing his intent to finish the job, was enough to make her feel vulnerable. She saw Aisha Hussin rally her father's army to her call, guns popping off round after round against her two monoliths, with little more effect than a mosquito on an elephant's back, but insects can be a nuisance. She twisted her hand, concentrated on the tectonics deep below. 'More. More.' Small piles of sand and rock the height of a man clumped together in pockets flanking Aisha's troops. Silently they engaged, sucking each screaming soldier down underground like quicksand.

'What is this work of hell?' shouted a gunman next to Aisha, sweat beading through his thick black beard. He rattled a few rounds into the nearest human mud mound, shards of rock coming loose, but failing to stop its advance until Aisha's blade neatly struck its neck.

'Aim for their heads,' she ordered, the headless body of earth collapsing in front of her. 'That satchel – what's in it?' she pointed.

'Grenades.' The gunman aimed his rifle at two more rumbling figures emerging from near his feet.

'You have a detonator?'

'Of course.'

'Give the bag to me.' Aisha commanded. 'Get the men to hold these creatures off for as long as possible.'

'Where are you going, Miss Hussin?'

Aisha looked over at Adam's fighters. One of the three golems was smashing through the Sacred Band ranks and heading towards Gary Willis and Geraint South on the apex of what was left standing of Mount Sinai. 'Detonator please, soldier.'

Another pulse of white light came from Geraint's sword just as Gary swung his, shaving a slice of rock from the golem's huge fist as it crashed down from above. The two staggered back. 'We won't hold it by ourselves,' South shouted, readying for another attack. Willis found his feet again and athletically leapt up the sliding steps of the mountainside straight onto the golem's upper arm. 'What are you doing, Gary?' Geraint flapped in a panic.

'Keep this thing focused on you, Geraint!' Gary yelled as he plunged his sword into the elbow joint. He glanced over his shoulder and saw Aisha sprinting up from behind them, fending off a few smaller earthmen with brute strength. Geraint fired his knight light once more, its light bouncing off the golem's torso, causing it to lose balance slightly. Aisha slipped between its legs as it buckled and dropped the satchel beneath it.

'Gary. Jump!' Aisha cried, squeezing the trigger of the detonator. The explosion of rock catapulted Willis into flight, landing harshly on his side. Fragments of stone and soil showered on the three of them.

'Impressive.' Fernando popped his head up from his hiding place back in the alcove, coughing through the smoke.

'Might not be enough unless we can stop Lady Morgan,' Aisha said despondently, noticing the shards of rock already reforming into the golem's shape. 'Come on Luke, Violet. Bring her down.'

Crouching behind an uprooted tree, Violet tried to gauge the distance between her and Lady Morgan. It was only a few metres. 'I can make a run for it, grab the Necklace of Harmonia as I did before,' she turned to Luke. He cast a frown.

'Too risky, Violet. She'll see you coming. Wait…' his train of thought was interrupted with the arrival of Sir Lawrence. His charge towards his wife had slowed to a trot as he came closer to her flowing silver gown. He raised his lone sword directly at her, Luke straining to hear his words.

'Morgan. No more. Whatever world you had planned, it is clear I was to be no part of it. Nor were my men.' Sir Lawrence permitted a quiver of emotion in his voice. 'My loyalty to you, and those before me, has been nothing more than a platform for you to seek omnipotence. You may undo wider faiths, replace gods and deities with you at the centre, but it will only ever be *you,* won't it. Never *us.*'

'As it was for many millennia, my love. Spirits of nature born to be both feared and admired by mankind. My sister and I, the true masters of fate among your wretched people, reduced to fantasies and legend. You, Sir Lawrence Worthington, Knight of Lancelot, might find peace in such a world – I most certainly cannot.' Lady Morgan cowered, still holding Sir Lawrence's gaze. She held his second sword and offered the hilt to him. 'Your bloodline has always had my respect, Sir Lawrence. That should suffice,' she said coldly.

Now was their chance, Luke thought. He tapped Violet on the shoulder and whispered 'Try and get close enough to the Necklace, and when I say so, grab it from that hag's throat.' Violet began to inch forward as Luke revealed himself to Lady Morgan and Sir Lawrence. 'Hey! Lover's quarrel over there,' he chirped. 'I realise I'm interrupting but I'm guessing, Morgan, that this is still important?' he brandished the Palladium, teasing. Lady Morgan's face turned ashen, her eyes checking the space around her in disbelief.

'The Palladium! Get it for me, Lawrence. Now.' Lady Morgan cried hysterically. Sir Lawrence simply stood in quiet acknowledgement of Luke's superior position when he glimpsed Excalibur poised in his hand, ready to strike. 'Do it, Master Allen. For the good of us all,' he thought.

'Violet. Now!' Luke yelled as Excalibur's blade sliced through the Palladium, shattering it into pieces in a spark of pure firelight. Lady Morgan grasped her breast in anguish just as Violet Butcher sprang out at her side, wrapped her delicate hand over the Necklace of Harmonia and pulled it with all she could muster. In a fit of rage, Lady Morgan propelled her back with sharp green energy, smacking Violet's head back on the rocks. As she brushed her ponytail away from her face she tasted iron blood in her mouth, trickling down from her nose.

'I can learn too, young Knight of Bors,' Lady Morgan cackled, as another bolt of energy shot from her hand and threw Luke to the ground. She twisted her wrist gently, summoning the soil and roots around Luke to envelop him, severing him from Excalibur. 'So foolish. This cannot be the future of the Round Table,' she sighed.

'Violet!' Luke cried out, his voice slowly muffled under the earth. He gestured to Excalibur, his hand being pulled further away. Violet crawled to the blade and wrapped her fingers around its handle, felt an instant burning throughout every muscle. She collapsed to her chest in agony. Lady Morgan stooped over her menacingly, Sir Lawrence's second blade twitching in anticipation.

'Dear child, what do you know of love and sacrifice? So young, so innocent.' Lady Morgan mocked. 'Not your time yet, alas, and it may never be.' She brought Sir Lawrence's sword high, and Violet squeezed her eyes shut, awaiting her fate. When she opened them, she saw the frozen face of Sir Lawrence Worthington, his own sword blade protruding out from his ribs and a breath away from Violet. Foam and blood welled from his mouth, but he managed a subtle wink as he sighed his last. As William Wood had done before, to spare her life from Colonel Stephen Thorpe in Edinburgh, impelling Mack Benson to a sacrifice that at the time she couldn't have hoped to comprehend – this act, together with that of her father Nick – surged through Violet like the warmth of the sun. Without hesitation, she pushed Sir Lawrence's body to one side and thrust the tip of the king's blade straight into the heart of the glowing red jewel around Lady Morgan's neck. A shrill sound split the air around her, the deep ruby colour wept from the cracked Necklace down through Excalibur's steel into Violet herself. Her lungs filled to their limit, then her eyes closed, shutting out Lady Morgan's terrifying screams.

The bonds around Luke began to loosen. He twisted his body free and scrambled over to Violet. He shook her. 'Violet. Violet. Come on. Please,' he begged, whispering to himself, to no effect. Excalibur lay by her side, still gleaming. He seized its pommel and turned to face Lady Morgan. The sorceress held her face in her hands as she did in King Arthur's tomb, the Necklace of Harmonia destroyed, and with it, her youth and life force.

'Now die, you bitch!' Luke bellowed with a swing of the king's blade to Lady Morgan's head. Beams of pale green light shone from where it had struck her temple, her face taut with terror, aged skin stretched over bone. She still stood. A thump of energy deep into Luke's stomach pushed him back to the ground, amazed. He stared at Excalibur in disbelief, then back at the ghoulish figure of Lady Morgan, her eyes hollow, jaw sagging. 'Impossible. If this can't kill her, what can?' he fretted.

Lady Morgan's fingers became like sharpened claws, slashing

each side of Luke as he evaded his tormentor. He flung Excalibur once more, nicked one of Lady Morgan's arms, still she advanced. 'Min. Minnie. Come on, love – give me something here,' he pleaded with himself once more. He had run out of options as he backed against the uprooted tree, trapped. He pricked his forearm against the sharpened split bark, drawing blood. *'Nature's way.'* Mary Cassidy's words flooded back to the forefront of his mind. He held Excalibur's tip down, kneeling before Lady Morgan as she went in for the kill, the glint of its blade reverting to a shortened wooden thorn. As the witch threw herself at Luke, impaling herself on the staff, he thrust it upwards for good measure. 'Got you – bitch!' he hissed through his teeth. Lady Morgan could only groan softly as her body crumbled to ash around him, carried away on a breeze. Luke slouched back and closed his eyes for a moment. He let out a dull chuckle. 'Why do you always make me think for myself, Minnie?' The mountain began to settle, the crash of spent golems was met with the cheers of Sacred Band warriors and remaining gunmen, the cries of *Lions* and *Palamedes* echoing all around.

Adam appeared and broke his brother's momentary peace. 'You OK?' he asked. Rays of pure sunlight began to break apart the dark clouds above. Violet tried to sit upright and uttered a few curse words quite unbecoming of her, rubbing her bloodied nose.

'Yeah. Think we'll be fine.' Luke smiled.

CHAPTER 26

━━━━◆━━━━

BATH, ENGLAND

27th July 2012 AD

BUNTING DRESSED UP THE LIMESTONE STREETS IN THE RED, WHITE and blue of the Union Jack. A local street artist drew an audience on the corner of Parade Gardens as he completed a vibrant chalk sketch of the Olympic rings and stylised sportsmen and women celebrated from games past. Aisha glanced up at the solemn-looking rain cloud darkening the Mendip hills beyond. 'Please don't let it rain,' she prayed in earshot of Violet, who sat across the table sipping her coffee.

'Can you imagine how gutted that guy would be? He's been working on that sketch for hours. One downpour and it's ruined.' Violet gave a cheeky smile.

'Probably not as gutted as they would be in London right now. Not sure if that stadium even has a roof,' Aisha replied. 'Suppose the weather is the one thing that we can't control.' Violet carefully placed her coffee cup back down, wiped cappuccino foam from her top lip and took a look at her watch.

'What time did Luke and Adam say they'd join us?' she asked.

'About 3.00 pm.' Aisha checked her phone. 'Luke's messaged us, saying they're running late. Typical.'

The table was wobbly, each movement either of them made rocked it off-kilter. Violet's wooden staff slid off, but she caught it before it hit the ground. 'Damn. Not sure I'm going to get used to having this thing around all the time. Pretty sure I'm going to leave it behind somewhere,' she muttered.

Aisha placed her hand firmly around her own staff. 'I don't know... I'm growing to like mine. Certainly useful for long walks and pushing past people in queues,' she laughed. 'Then, of course, you can always fend off boys that try to give you... well, any unwanted attention.' Violet bit her bottom lip with a blush.

'Would Luke allow any unwanted attention from other boys?' Violet teased.

'Probably not. Still, he's pretty clueless,' Aisha playfully replied. She and Luke had grown so close over this past month, to the point where it was impossible to try and hide it from the others. Luke had spent several days away with her and her friend Bushra back in London, then settled in Richard's old home in Bath. Adam, recognising the two needed space, decided to retreat to The Bear Pub, now reopened with the help of Beth and its new owner, Violet Butcher. Aisha had broken the news to them all just last week that plans were afoot to travel back to Jordan and be with her extended family. Whether the move was a permanent one or not had not been disclosed. Violet was desperate to ask, but could never find the opportune moment until now.

'Will you... will you come back? To Bath? You and Luke?' Violet's voice quivered in fear of the response. Aisha reached across and took her hand.

'Us knights have got to stick together, right, daughter of Sir Bors?' Aisha soothed.

'Daughter of Sir Palamedes,' Violet playfully replied. She relaxed in the comfort of Aisha's promise that she would see her hazel eyes again. It was just a matter of when. 'I hope when we do, it won't be quite like before.' She gripped Aisha's hand in reply. 'Not sure I can go through something like all this again. Losing family, losing friends… losing…' she trailed off as if the words were too painful to express. Aisha sat upright, concern spreading across her face.

'Violet, you know Luke cares for you too, right? I'm not ever going to take him from you.' Aisha spoke sharply. 'You've become so close recently, the Allen boys are your family and…'

'It's not Luke,' Violet interrupted, offering a direct look at Aisha, only to break away almost ashamedly. She need say no more to her, but confidently withdrew her hand. Aisha composed herself and switched subjects.

'What was it like, wielding Excalibur?' she asked. Violet became more settled.

'Strange. I felt unstoppable, but also, terrified. Of what I could do with it I mean. Part of me wanted to listen to it, never let it go, then another part couldn't let go quick enough.' She lost herself in her thoughts.

'I'd say it's that last part that allowed you to wield it in the first place,' Aisha proposed. 'No good in the hands of a selfish egomaniac.'

'Wonder if that's what Mack Benson and Luke felt as well?' Violet replied. Aisha gave a little shrug.

'Hopefully so. If King Arthur could do it, I'm sure Luke will manage,' came Aisha's lighter tone. She looked over at the Putney Bridge, the slip of the River Avon just catching the afternoon light. 'He'd better be able to,' she thought to herself.

❧

'So this is what millions of people from around the world come to see each year, is it? A small, dirty pond.' Luke muttered to Adam as the two sat beside the Roman Baths, watching tourists pose and take selfies against the vivid green waters.

'It shouldn't be dirty, Luke.' Adam sighed back.

'Looks dirty. Doesn't smell great either.'

'Probably the minerals in it. Romans and Celts used to think they were healing.'

'Is that why they all lived to the grand old age of fifty,' Luke scoffed, skipping a loose stone into the pool, promptly rebuked by his brother for doing so. 'Whose face is that supposed to be?' he pointed to the stone relief carvings of a delicate female form. 'Seen a few around here.'

'That's Minerva, supposedly. Roman form of the Greek Goddess Athena... which you of course now know all about.' Adam informed him. 'Much of Bath was built in worship of her, for her wisdom and beauty. Its Roman name was Aqua Sulis, hence all the dirty water, as you put it,' he nodded in different directions.

'Minerva? *Min-erva?*' Luke paused in thought.

'I know. That hadn't escaped me either.' Adam turned the corner of his mouth up. 'More to Mary Cassidy than just your nickname for her perhaps.' Luke remained silent. He placed the wooden staff of Excalibur on his lap and took a deep breath.

'You sure we should do this, bro?' Luke asked. 'I know the Palladium is destroyed, and, thanks to Violet, the Necklace of Harmonia too. But what if...?'

'What if what?' Adam queried sternly.

'You know. There's a lot of trouble in this world, only need to switch on the news or read a paper.' Luke stuttered.

'When was the last time you read a paper, Luke?'

'Knock it off, wise-ass! You know what I mean.'

Adam stood and put a strong palm on his brother's shoulder. 'I know, brother, I know. But every line of Sir Bedivere knew to return Excalibur to its rightful place, whether that was Arthur's Seat in Edinburgh or someplace else where the Lady of the Lake could find it, know it was safe. Keeping hold of it never ends well, as King Arthur discovered. Sooner or later its need for blood will require more than just the ultimate sacrifice. I fear even those with the utmost devoted love for others would be corrupted in time - just as with the Necklace of Harmonia. You must return it.'

Luke digested his brother's words and knew they made complete sense, as they so often did. The two had thought hard about where it might be best to cast the king's blade back to the waters. With King Arthur's tomb destroyed and Tintagel bearing too many scars for

Luke over Mary's apparent demise, somewhere closer to home, more meaningful to their father and his closest friends William Wood, Karen Milligan, Nick Butcher and Mack Benson – all of whom had their ashes or ceremonial tributes offered at this very site – appeared to be the logical choice. He offered the tip of the staff to the lime-washed pool, standing there feeling stupid for several minutes before a familiar hand shot out and grabbed it. Luke stumbled back into Adam's arms in shock.

'Why thank you, hun. Knew you'd come good in the end.' Mary smiled, hair flowing down longer than Luke ever knew it, sapphire blue dress leaving her slender neck and upper breast bare. She looked as beautiful as when Luke first met her climbing out of the Harvard swimming pool after training. Effortless charm. 'I'll take this off your hands, for now.'

'Min. I mean, Mary... babe,' Luke stuttered. 'Aren't people going to see you?' he looked all around at the growing numbers of visitors.

'Not to worry, Luke. Only you two boys can. Smart little trick I've learnt. It'll just be between you guys and me – you can keep a secret now right?' Mary grinned.

'Is it over? Morgan le Fay and all?' Luke asked.

'She's at peace now, hun, that's all that matters. You can no more stop the earth than you can stop the water, but for now at least, she's at peace.' Mary gave a soft look.

'She could come back though?' Adam queried.

'Just as a felled tree can send up shoots again, of course. But it won't necessarily grow the same way. As I said, though, I'll take this for now. Should you need Excalibur again, you'll know.' came Mary's gentle reply.

'How?' Luke interjected bluntly.

'Ah, son of Sir Galahad, you'll always know where to find me. I told you, always at home in the water.' Mary transformed the wooden staff into the gleaming blade of Excalibur one final time. 'Unfortunately, with the Benson line at a bit of a loose end right now following poor Mack's demise and the loss of his only heir to Sir

Bedivere, the burden of this blade will fall to you… for now at least. Sure you'll be up to the challenge though?' Mary teased.

Luke puffed his chest out and gave a reassuring cough of approval. 'I destroyed the Palladium, that's got to be a good thing, right?'

'Indeed it is, hun. Only took two thousand years, but someone finally had the courage to. Who would have thought it would have been a dopey drop-out like you?' chuckled Mary.

'And the Necklace of Harmonia, young Violet took care of that,' Luke continued. Mary raised a quizzical eyebrow.

'Morgan le Fay was certainly right about that one. More than just a daughter of Sir Bors, a daughter of Ares as well, just like the original wearer of the Necklace. Your kin might have some serious competition, Adam,' she said, admiring the gleam of Excalibur's blade. Adam tried to take stock, the notion that Violet could follow the same path as him, take a lover of the same sex and fight by her side, both Knight of the Round Table and Sacred Band, empowered by a cornerstone of the Trinity. It was unfathomable, uncontrollable even. He got goosebumps at the thought. 'The gods are always playing games with us. Don't let such worry consume you, Adam. Try just to play along as best you can.' Mary bowed graciously. She turned to leave when Luke seized her arm.

'Min, me and Aisha… we…' he stumbled.

'I know, hun. Perfect choice, the Round Table should be family. You have my blessing, and Jenny Van Hansen's.' Mary calmed him as she slipped her arm free.

'Mary…' Adam waded waist-deep into the water, pushing his brother aside abruptly.

'I really must be going, Adam.'

'But you… will you be forgotten?'

'What do you mean?'

'I mean, what Lady Morgan spoke of, that fear she had. We all stop believing in you and your kind, in favour of new beliefs. What if… what if…' Adam was now struggling to string his words together cogently.

'Iain Donnelly really got to you, didn't he.' Mary gave a slow but warming blink. Adam could only stare at his submerged feet. 'Truth is, the memory of one is as powerful as the memory of a million, Adam. If you remember, as your father and mother did, then we'll never be gone.' She smiled again. She turned her back once more, dipping Excalibur beneath the surface as the water reached her neck. 'And remember, Adam, religions are not weapons, and never will be at their heart, they don't wound like a sword or spear, or a lover. That's all human. And no two humans are the same... Always have faith.'

With a quick splash, Mary had gone. A tour guide shouted at Adam and Luke for standing in the ancient baths and ordered the two out immediately. They darted for the exit.

CHAPTER 27

⊰◆⊱

BATH, ENGLAND

27th July 2012 AD

L UKE KNOTTED HIS JUMPER AROUND HIS WAIST AND TRIED TO PAT his legs dry. 'Gary's going to kill us if any of that goes viral online.' He cursed.

'Think it happens quite a lot here. In fact, Gary said the Bath Chronicle took to listing all the incidents when tourists and the occasional hippy tried to force their way into the baths for a quick dip, despite the health risks. Was one of the reasons they opened the ThermaSpa over there, probably.' Adam gestured to the polished new block opposite.

'Well, that one looks warmer,' Luke tutted, with his fingers pressed firmly under his arms. 'We're late for Aisha and Violet, you realise.' The two made their way across the Abbey Courtyard towards the River, Adam tapping his phone to check for any messages from Gary Willis or Geraint South just in case. There was a reassuring sense of accomplishment having the two sides of the Round Table together once more, the Red and White Dragons united in a common purpose to hold the miscreants of the world to account. Even with relics such as the Palladium and Necklace of Harmonia out of the picture, both Willis and South were adamant others existed. Pooling their extensive connections and resources was only logical, even

139

if the two argued incessantly about the merits of journalism over historical study. A picture message popped up, a beaming Fernando smeared with both the British and Italian flag colours, one on each cheek, a decoration shared by Chris Wood and a few recognised Sacred Band members jostling for a positon in the background. The caption read 'Hope you're ready, General Allen – Opening Ceremony at 9.00 pm.' Adam responded with a simple 'You Bet' before easing the phone back into his pocket. His family had indeed grown.

'Adam... I think we're being followed.' Luke nudged his brother sharply, shepherding him under one of the buttresses of the Abbey.

'What? How do you know?' Adam asked.

'Trust me. Enough time around the college campus,' Luke replied. Adam gave a disapproving look. He turned back. All appeared clear. 'Trust me,' Luke said again.

'I think I'd know, too, Luke.' Adam rebuked. 'Spent a bit of time in war zones, you know, and while not quite the carnage of a dormitory frat party I think I could...' his sarcasm was halted by the presence of a brutish, lone figure dressed in khaki. His head was shaved, the skin weathered. Adam deduced a military pedigree from his formal posture and haggard expression; special forces perhaps.

'Luke and Adam Allen. Been a while.' The man offered his hand in introduction, neither brother accepting it. 'It's OK, it has been a while, I know,' he sighed with remorse. 'I came to pay my respects to your father. Word did reach me by Gary Willis about Richard. I didn't know how best to react, or indeed whether I would be welcome. Perhaps I should have thought it through.'

Luke cocked his head to the side and scanned the gentleman from top to bottom, the resemblance becoming more and more clear. 'Alex? Uncle Alex?' Only vague fragments of memory came to him. The man gave a firm nod.

'Good to see you, Luke, so well at least. Last time I saw you, you were only ten I believe. You look a lot like Elaine.' Alex cracked a smile, which faded quickly when he turned to Adam. 'You, on the other hand, Adam, couldn't be more like your father. Easy to spot you in a crowd.'

Adam was quick to dispense with any pleasantries. 'We had no ashes for Richard. Nor did we have his… staff. So Luke and I burned a piece of Glastonbury Thorn in his memory, same with Mack Benson, scattered them in the Roman Baths over there. We'd go in with you, but we're probably barred for life,' he snapped impatiently, contempt in his every word. Luke dug a subtle elbow into his brother's ribs, urging respect.

Alex brought his hands together and placed his chin on his chest. 'Thank you, that was decent of you both. And sorry about your mother. I hadn't seen Elaine for such a long time, but she was always in my thoughts.'

'That's great, Uncle. Luke and I need to be going. As I said, you're welcome to pay your respects and…' Adam was jerked to one side by Luke.

'Bro, come on. I know you're angry about everything right now, about Dad, Iain the whole lot. But Alex is family, and he's here with us. Plus, he's a Sacred Band member, isn't he? Just like you,' Luke insisted.

'Allegedly.' Adam scoffed.

'So… doesn't that make him an ally? Your ally? Let's be honest, you could do with some mentoring now Father's gone, and if Uncle Alex has seen frontline action, he could be good for you?' Luke proposed. Adam remained unconvinced until his brother spoke the words 'Have some faith in people again bro,' as if Mary Cassidy herself were standing there in front of him once more. He scratched the back of his neck and heaved a heavy sigh before turning back to his uncle and offering his hand.

'We're just meeting some friends for coffee, and running late. Did you want to join us, Alex?' Adam asked, maintaining a harsh edge to his voice.

'I have an hour to kill before I need to leave for London. The Games have brought in just about every reserve soldier they can to help with security. Even crippled ones like me.' Alex accepted graciously.

'You don't look injured,' Luke said in mild admiration for the impressive build of a gentleman who must be of a similar age to their father. Alex responded with a tap of his finger on his temple and sorrow across his brow. Plenty of time for that later, Luke thought.

Aisha and Violet waved from the café across the road, Aisha playfully pointing at her watch with a mocking shake of her head. Luke jogged on ahead, arms stretched out in apology.

'Where were you stationed?' Adam asked Alex.

'Iraq. Gulf War in 1990. Was only twenty years old when I did my first tour. Thought I had the measure of it, given the powers we both share. Nothing was going to stop me, not even your father. Richard begged me not to go but I was so determined to do our family proud, the Sacred Band proud, him proud, my older brother. Hell, even fell for the whole jingoist propaganda that was doing the rounds back then,' Alex replied.

'Some things never change.' Adam mused.

'Indeed. Richard always used to say nationalism meant putting your country above all others, whereas patriotism…'

'…was having the courage to sacrifice your country for the benefit of all others. He told me that too,' Adam finished. 'Did you have a partner?' he enquired.

'I thought I did. Turned out not to be. Suppose I was all the weaker for it.' Alex expressed. 'You?' he asked tenderly.

'Turned out not to be.' Adam paused briefly before responding.

'I'm guessing you've seen quite a few things for such a young age. Especially if Richard was involved. I'd like to hear about them. When we have time,' Alex hinted.

Adam watched his brother embrace Aisha and Violet. He gripped his wrist and felt the warmth of blue fire through his fingers. 'We'll have time.'

THE SACRED BAND TRINITY: GRAIL
THE END.

ABOUT THE AUTHOR

JAMES MACTAVISH BRINGS HIS LOVE OF MYTHOLOGY AND HISTORY together in gripping short stories that transport the reader from present day events to the antiquities of Ancient Greece and Arthurian legend. Having been inspired by several works focusing on what it is to be a gay man in the 21st Century - the journey of coming out, finding your place and living life to the full - MacTavish challenges the cultural stereotypes of this genre and instead presents his audience with 'heroes'. Characters that can inspire and lead, not just be accepted. The imaginative stories are deeply researched with creative flair, focusing on the themes of loyalty, duty and the love of family. As a keen competitive swimmer and open water enthusiast, expect references to an individual's strength and discipline whist championing the notion that sometimes, to be different is to be better.

Lightning Source UK Ltd.
Milton Keynes UK
UKHW012217140421
382011UK00001B/32